# Hunt:
# Red Riding Hood Retold

## DEMELZA CARLTON

A tale in the Romance a Medieval Fairy Tale series

# DEDICATION

In memory of Snorri Sturluson, a medieval twister of
tales and mythology.

# *One*

"Once upon a time, a king fell in love with the goddess of love. They were very happy together, and she bore him a son.

"Though he had many older sons by his previous wives, she wanted him to name this child his heir. But the king did not.

"This king worshipped an ancient god of the forest, who had protected his kingdom for generations, and he prayed daily at the god's altar.

"One day, when he was at his prayers, his goddess wife came to find him. Instead of praying like he usually did, the king had her son lying on top of the altar, and the king beseeched his god to take the boy as his servant, to better protect the kingdom.

"The goddess was incensed – the boy was hers, he did not belong to some god of trees – so she snatched the child up in her arms. Only to discover that the boy no longer drew breath – the king had sacrificed him to his barbaric god, who relished such things.

"She raised her hand to strike the king dead, as he had struck her son, but the king's youngest son, whose mother had died birthing him, came running in, and wrapped himself about the queen's legs, for he saw her as the only mother he had known, and loved both her and his little brother dearly.

"The king feared for his son, and begged for the boy's life.

"The queen – not just a goddess, but a powerful sorceress, too – called down a terrible storm. The raging winds destroyed the palace, and lightning struck each of the king's sons, killing them instantly. All but the youngest, who she allowed to live.

"The king she turned into a white wolf, so pale the shepherds of his flocks instantly saw him coming, and chased him away until he vanished into the deep woods, high into the mountains.

"The youngest son became king, building a new capital closer to the trade routes, and he ushered in a time of great prosperity for the kingdom, because he was greatly favoured by both his father's god and the goddess of love, his stepmother.

"She favoured him so much that she allowed him to marry one of her own daughters by her new lover, and both king and queen were very happy and had many children.

"But the old king, the white wolf…he stayed in the mountains, hidden from humans, until the worst winter snows covered the towns. Only then would he venture out, his white fur blending perfectly with the snow, as he hunted for the enchantress who had killed his sons."

"But did he ever find her, Grandmother?" Rosa asked.

Grandmother flashed an enigmatic smile. "The tales never say, so I suppose he did not. Perhaps his time came, and he died, and that's where his story ends."

Rosa wrinkled her nose. "Or perhaps it is nothing more than a tale, and this king never truly lived at all."

"Perhaps," Grandmother agreed. She glanced out the window, where the late afternoon light was already turning the shutters rosy. "But it never hurts to be careful, especially on your way home through the forest. Practise your magic, too, on your way. I'm not sure what will fall first, snow or night, but you'd best be home before both. And don't forget to take the medicine for Edda. She might not last the winter, but we must help her all we can to see the spring."

Rosa thought of the ancient woman, who never left her cottage now. "Edda has seen many springs already. What good is one more?"

Another enigmatic smile. "When it might be your last, you will always fight for one more. One more season, one more day...perhaps even one more minute, for a lot can be said in that time. But I pray it is a long time before you know the truth of it in your heart. Now, go home, child, and don't forget your cloak, for you will need it in the snow."

"Yes, Grandmother." Rosa lifted the brand new cloak her grandmother had given her only hours before, and flung it around her shoulders. The fine red wool hung heavily, so that none but the strongest gust of wind could disturb it. It was the cloak of a lady or a princess, not a carpenter's daughter. All her other cloaks had been brown, to match her humble station. To wear something so rich and vibrant seemed to scream for attention from the very heavens themselves.

"The village needs to see you for what you are, for one day, when I am gone, you will be their witch, and they will need to know who to come to," Grandmother said, as if reading her thoughts.

If she was simply a healer, a woman who knew her herbs, it would be fine, but if the town knew her magic was the elemental kind, and far more powerful than her grandmother's…Rosa gulped. The other girls already thought her strange. If they knew what she could do…

"Be off with you, child! And practise!" Grandmother shooed her out of the house.

# *Two*

For the first time in his life, Chase didn't know what to do. Now Maja was gone, and Abraham, too, he was all alone in the world. But one thing was certain: the king had made it clear he could not stay here. So, he would depart.

Chase sold Abraham's horse for a good price, and tucked the coins into the pouch at his waist. He had enough money to get him to almost any kingdom in the civilised world, and for the first time in his life, he was free to choose who he served.

King Erik's court in Aros was famed for its tourneys, and he could win any archery contest with his eyes closed. Perhaps it was time to aim high and attach himself to a royal court, to see how his fortunes fared there. Better than his brother's fortune, he'd wager, for Heber's land was not so fruitful of late, or so his last letter had said.

Yes, he would go to Aros.

There was nothing left for him here.

Sir Chase mounted his mare, and set off on his quest for fame and fortune.

# *Three*

Rosa hurried home. She told herself it was because of the lateness of the hour, but in her heart she knew the truth. Her wild imagination had been so caught up in her grandmother's tale that more than once, she fancied she saw a shadow lurking behind the trees, following her home.

She tried to distract herself by practising, as her grandmother had said, but her magic didn't seem to want to cooperate today. Snow started falling, too, and she couldn't be sure if the flurries were her powers at work, or the natural movement of the breeze.

Snow already lay thick on the ground in the village by the time she reached it. She reached for the door of her family's cottage.

"Lule, I told you to put down your sewing and cut up the vegetables for the soup!" Mother scolded.

"Why can't Rosa do it?" Lule whined.

"Because she's still at your grandmother's, and if the snow keeps falling like this, she might not be home until morning. Your father's bringing fresh straw for our beds, and as soon as he gets home, I'll be busy dealing with that. Do you want supper or don't you?"

"Yes, Mother."

Rosa drew her hand back under her cloak. She hated cutting onions, and there were always so many for the soup. Let Lule do it for once. Rosa could take her grandmother's package to Edda in the meantime. Maybe when she came back, the soup would be ready and she wouldn't have to make it this time.

# Four

Sir Chase rode through the gates, sparing a nod of approval for the stout construction of the King of Aros' castle. The thickness of the walls spoke of the kingdom's strength, while the gaily coloured clothing of those who walked within its walls whispered of wealth. Service here would suit him well.

A groom appeared to take care of his horse, and Chase dismounted. He lingered long enough to throw his saddlebags over his own shoulder before allowing the beast to be led off. He'd heard the telltale thwack of arrows in the practice range, and he fancied taking a shot of his own. One that would reach the ears of the queen.

In one gate, out another, and he found the practice field, where a trio of men at arms took their turns at a target. They certainly needed the practice – none had managed to hit more than the outer circle of the target. Chase's father would not have tolerated such sloppy shots, especially at that distance. Why, he stood three times the distance as they did from the target, and he had the perfect shot.

His bow was off his back and in his hands before he'd finished the thought. He strung it with the ease of practice, and plucked an arrow from his quiver. He drew, sighted, breathed and loosed, his thoughts following the arrow's flight between the three men, then across the field to sink squarely into the centre of the target.

Exclamations of horror came from the men as they turned to find the source of the arrow, which turned to words of wonder at the size of his bow and the strength it must take to wield it.

Chase held it out. "Here, you try," he offered. The bow was taller than the man who took it from him. But Chase thought the stocky guard might have the strength to draw it, all the same.

A pleasant afternoon of archery ensued. Chase could definitely get used to this. Maybe even call Aros home.

The sound of a throat clearing drew Chase's attention and that of his companions.

"Sir Knight, Her Majesty, Queen Margareta, requests your presence at dinner in the Great Hall," the herald said.

Chase grinned. "I'd be honoured. Is there anywhere I might bathe and make myself presentable to greet Her Majesty?"

"An apartment has been prepared. Follow me, Sir Knight."

"It's Chase. Sir Chase," Chase said.

The herald breathed a sigh of relief. "Sir Chase. Whence have you come, Sir Chase?"

Chase considered. Who knew how far word had spread about Abraham? He did not dare risk it. "I have travelled from lands so far away I doubt you have heard of them," he said grandly.

The herald's eyes widened. "Are you a Crusader, sir? Or have you come from the Holy Land? Have you fought in many battles?"

Chase chose the truth. "Many battles indeed." Fought with his brothers and Abraham in the courtyard, with sticks and then swords. Abraham had always bested him with a sword. Ah, but he would miss the man, brother in all but blood.

"His Majesty, King Erik, is fond of tales of battle. Perhaps he will ask you to regale us at dinner," the herald said.

"I fear I am no bard, or teller of tales. I speak best with sword and bow," Chase said.

The herald led the way inside. "Then you must tell what you can to one of the Queen's bards, so that he may tell the tale."

Tell Abraham's story? Who would believe it? Chase himself barely believed it, and he'd seen most of it with his own eyes. Enough to know the truth when Abraham had told him the rest.

He only had to look at his tourney armour to be reminded, for after many jugs of ale, he'd persuaded Abraham to lay his hands on the well-crafted leather. Now it was as beautiful as it was useless, for Abraham's warning that gold would be too soft for combat proved only too true. But if it would buy him a place in the royal court of Aros, he would consider his armour a small price to pay.

# Five

It was nigh on midnight by the time Rosa left Edda's cottage, full of far more than soup. It had been the old woman's name day, and every member of her family had visited her with gifts and blessings. Edda had insisted Rosa eat some of the cakes Edda's toothless maw could no longer devour, and tell her what they tasted like.

Then she'd prepared the medicinal tea her grandmother had sent, and read to Edda from the great bible the Baron himself had sent her. Tales of men rising from the dead, when even the weakest witch knew such things were not possible. Magic could only accomplish so much.

When Edda's eyes drifted shut and she began to snore, Rosa dared to close the book and set it back on the table. Rosa wrapped her cloak around herself and set out for home.

Halfway there, she wished she'd brought a lantern, for the cloudy sky and blowing snow made it too dark to see, but the wind would have only blown it out. Fortunately, the cold meant everyone kept their fires burning through the night, and enough light peeped through the gaps in the shutters that she could discern the houses.

Even if she hadn't lived in the village her whole life, she'd have known her family cottage by the smell of soup – evidently Lule had made it, with some to spare. She pushed the door open, careful to make as little noise as possible, and closed it behind her.

Rosa frowned. The fire burned low in the grate – as though no one had stoked it before going to bed. Strange. And the soup still hung over the coals, bubbling sluggishly. That wasn't normal, either. Inside, the smell of soup was so strong it was almost overpowering, but there was a whiff of something else lurking beneath it, too. Something…rotten.

Like the Baron's slaughterhouse close to Midsummer feast day.

Ah, it was late. She could help her mother search for the offending piece of meat in the morning, when it was lighter. Now, she should rekindle the fire, set the soup somewhere to cool, then head up to bed.

She threw a handful of kindling on the coals, then grabbed a cloth to unhook the cauldron from the fire. She could barely lift it – why, the cauldron was almost full, as if her family had prepared dinner, then not eaten it.

Rosa felt the air behind her shift, almost imperceptibly, and whirled to face whatever had caused it, swinging the cauldron around with her.

Soup splashed out, covering the enormous, ghostly shape that was there one moment, before it retreated into the darkness again.

Rosa seized a torch and thrust it into the fire until the pitch caught, then turned to face whatever it was.

Blue eyes burned in the darkness, where someone crouched low, ready to spring. Someone, or something?

"Show yourself," Rosa hissed, hoping she sounded braver than she felt. "I said show yourself, coward!"

She hadn't imagined it. Something huge and white came soaring out of the shadows. Something with teeth bigger than any human she'd ever seen.

Rosa's grip tightened on her torch, splinters digging into her fingers, but she didn't care. The oozing blood would be the monster's undoing, not hers, as she summoned her magic and swung the torch.

The flaming end of the torch collided with the creature, and a gust of air came from nowhere, adding power to the blow so that it carried the creature past Rosa and into the fireplace itself, where the flames blazed to life.

The creature yelped, then howled, as it struggled to get up with its white fur on fire. A streak of orange and white and red, it fled for the door, hitting it with such force that the door flew open, releasing the beast into the blizzard outside.

Rosa blinked, trying to make sense of what she'd seen. In her mind's eye, it had been a giant, white wolf, like something out of a fairytale. A scary fairytale.

A red and white wolf, her memory reminded her. The red of blood…

Her hand flew to her mouth as the leaping flames lit the scene she hadn't seen until now. A pair of feet stuck out from under the kitchen table, wearing Lule's house slippers. Father lay behind the door, blind eyes staring at the rafters as his hands seemed to reach for his throat, which was no longer there.

Mother lay facedown behind the woodpile, as if the creature had brought her down as she tried to run. Her neck, too, was a bloody ruin. Beside her was a basket of straw, which had started to smoke. Sparked by the beast running past her with its fur ablaze.

Even as she hesitated, the basket flared up fully, flames licking at the curtains.

Rosa's weary mind was slow to make sense of it all. Her family was dead, some giant wolf had killed them, and now her home was on fire.

Her home was on fire. And filling with smoke.

If she didn't want to join them in death, she had to get out. Now.

Coughing, Rosa staggered for the door, pausing only to grab the poker. If the wolf waited for her outside, she'd take the bastard with her to hell for this.

But outside there was nothing but clean snow, with no sign of the beast, or anyone else, either.

"Fire!" she coughed out, hoping someone would hear her. "Fire! Help!"

Doors began to open along the street, spilling light out onto the snow.

But it was too late. By the time the sun rose the next day, all that remained of her family home was a burned out shell, where her family had breathed their last.

The other villagers headed home, to breakfast and all the normal things they did every day.

Rosa knelt in the ashes and swore an oath of

vengeance. The beast would die at her hand for what he'd stolen from her.

# Six

"Your Majesties, may I present to you, the renowned knight from far off lands, the hero of countless battles, the mighty Sir Chase!" the herald bellowed.

Glad his helmet hid his grin at such flowery exaggeration, Chase strode into the hall. His stupid armour turned his usually smooth stride into more of a stiff march, but no one seemed to notice his discomfort. Instead, all they seemed to want to stare, wide-eyed, as though they'd never seen a man in armour before.

The king – Erik, Chase reminded himself –

rose and announced, "On the morrow, we shall hold a tourney so that you may all test your skills against such a legendary hero – "

Whatever else he said was drowned out by cheers and toasts to the king's health as the hall erupted on either side of Chase.

When Chase finally reached the dais where the king sat, instinct told him to kneel, but he could not – his benighted armour wouldn't let him.

"Fool," the queen muttered, as if reading his thoughts.

Chase whipped off his helm.

A gasp drew his eye from the queen to a girl – a princess, perhaps? – further along the high table. She blushed. Definitely a princess, ripe for marriage to some rival kingdom. Before some handsome knight stole her heart and her virtue, too.

But seducing princesses would have to wait until his place here was assured. Chase bowed from the waist, praying his armour would not slice him in two.

"Your Majesty King Erik," he said. "I am honoured by your hospitality. I wish only to serve."

He knew he should reach for his sword and lay it at the king's feet as he knelt, but even if he could reach his sword, kneeling was beyond him. He thought quickly.

"I eagerly await tomorrow's tourney, for what better way to show a man's fighting prowess? Yet there is more to a knight than his sword," he continued.

The princess blushed redder than ever. Perhaps she knew more of such things than a maiden should.

Then the queen laughed.

And he could think of nothing but her. A hush fell over the hall, as it seemed every man there shared his thoughts.

Her mocking smile made him wonder once more if the queen could indeed read minds. "Pray continue, Sir Knight."

"As you wish, most beautiful queen." He wet his lips. Abraham had been the one with a way with words, especially when it came to women. He racked his brain for something that would impress the queen. "A true hero must keep his wits as sharp as his blade. His honour must shine as bright as his armour, and never be allowed to tarnish." Chase glimpsed a fly out of the corner of his eye, flicked away by the princess's impatient hand, and inspiration struck. He continued with more confidence: "So that if his liege or his lady is plagued by the most enormous monster or the tiniest gnat, he can dispatch it forthwith."

He turned to face the princess.

"Allow me, Your Majesty," he said.

He reached behind him for his bow, notched an arrow to the string and let it fly. His arrow lodged in one of the tapestries high above the princess's head, missing the fly completely. Not that anyone would know for sure without climbing the wall to examine his arrow.

Stupid armour.

He had the princess's attention for certain now. But he needed the queen to be equally impressed.

A fly circled the queen's head.

Chase drew another arrow. He'd only have one shot at this, and his aim had to be perfect. He breathed out and loosed.

His arrow arced up over the queen's head before embedding itself in the wax encrusting a lit candelabra at the back of the dais. The candles wobbled for a moment, but thankfully did not fall.

The fly, still unharmed, flew toward the princess, whose eyes met his. If the queen was a mindreader, so was her daughter. And the daughter knew he'd missed the fly twice.

He winked at her and said, "Fear not, young maiden. A knight's duty is to save every lady, not just the queen."

Chase reached for a third arrow.

The fly buzzed back toward the queen.

Chase released the arrow, just as the queen flicked her fingers to shoo the fly away.

His heart leaped into his throat. By all that was holy, please, no.

Queen Margareta leaped to her feet. "Guards!"

A thin line of blood trickled down the queen's fingers to where the arrow had lodged in the table before her. As if taunting him for his poorly timed shot, a shimmery wing was all that remained of the fly, now squashed under the weight of his arrow.

Chase didn't feel the guards seizing his arms – his armour was too thick for that – until the men started to drag him back, out of the hall.

No. This was all wrong. He was supposed to impress the queen, not shoot her.

"Your Majesty, I meant...I meant to rid you of a pest, not..." He was mortified to hear the weakness in his voice. Begging.

"Silence!" Queen Margareta thundered.

Chase had never been more relieved to obey a woman's command.

At her side, King Erik rose. "Anyone who seeks to harm my queen commits treason. Such a heinous crime is punishable by death."

No. He hadn't. He'd wanted to impress her, help her, not harm her. He'd never harm a woman. Never. Why, when his own sister lay dying, begging him to leave her to find her husband, to bring him home, Chase had not been able to release her hand. He'd learned archery so he could defend her. Like he wanted to serve this queen. Not…

"He's telling the truth!" The high, clear voice could only belong to the young princess.

She stood eye to eye with the queen over the head of the woman who sat between them. Her nurse, Chase presumed, for the woman was trying to make the princess sit down, but the girl was having none of it. "He shot a fly. Look!" The princess pointed.

A silent battle raged between mother and daughter.

Chase's own life rested on the outcome, he knew, but he couldn't think through his fascination at these two compelling women. The queen was formidable, but the princess did not fear her.

Whoever the girl married…he'd better not rule a rival kingdom, for that would mean war.

Somehow, the queen's eyes had moved back to Chase. Her voice was quiet but deadly. "Get out. This once, you may leave with your life. Set foot in this kingdom again and you will not be so lucky."

The princess had won, but he did not dare risk a glance of thanks in her direction, lest the queen change her mind.

He bowed, then fled, leaving his hopes in tatters on the flagstone floor.

# Seven

"There she goes! The witch! She murdered her family one Midwinter and drank their blood with the devil and that's where she gets her powers from. Don't look her in the eye or you'll be next!"

Children shrieked and ran. All but one – a boy of perhaps nine or ten years, who dared to look her in the eye.

"Witch!" he taunted, even as he ignored his own warning.

Rosa gritted her teeth, hefting her bag higher on her shoulder, and said nothing.

It would be so easy to summon a gust of wind to lift the boy off his feet and deposit him at the top of the nearest tree, or on the roof of his equally ignorant parents' cottage, but she would not use her power for something so petty.

But surely no one would blame her for closing her eyes for just a moment and imagining the boy's panicked screams as he sat in that tree or thatch, before he begged for her help in getting him down.

The whole village might hate her, taunt her, and whisper rumours that only children dared repeat in her hearing, but when they needed help, they would still come to the cottage, hat in hand, and she would give it.

Her grandmother's cottage in the woods, since the night her parents' home had burned, but it was the best place for her now.

For in the forest's isolation, she did not have to listen to the taunts every day.

"Ah, there you are! Are the boots as pretty as the Baron promised?" Grandmother asked, climbing laboriously to her feet and brushing the dirt from her skirt. She lived in the garden most days, talking more to her plants than she did to Rosa.

Rosa's heart sank. "I'm sorry, Grandmother, I forgot the boots. I was talking to Alard, who needs another of your elixirs, and I was so lost in thought when I left the Great House…"

Grandmother's eyes were sharp, seeing into Rosa's very soul. "Is that boy of the Baron's begetting more bastards? Who is it this time?"

Rosa sighed. "Piroska, who else? It seems he cannot help himself around her."

Grandmother snorted. "Oh, I think he helps himself all too readily, and that's the problem. He should marry the girl and be done with it. Not like anyone better will have him."

Did Rosa imagine it, or did Grandmother's eyes dart toward her as she said that? "The problem is that Alard still hopes, Grandmother. No matter what I say…he is adamant that the best baroness should be a skilled healer."

"Then I shall go into town to fetch my boots myself on the morrow, and have a word with the boy while I'm at it. The best baroness is one who'll give him babies, and Piroska's as fertile as they come. His father's not getting any younger, after all." Grandmother led the way into the house, holding the door open for Rosa.

Rosa followed her in, and thumped her sack on the table. "I remembered your honey, though. Now we should have enough to start a new batch of mead. I'll make a start on it on the morrow, when you go into town."

"You're not coming with me?"

More than ever, Grandmother's eyes seemed to read Rosa's soul.

"You're not in love with that silly boy, are you?"

Rosa shook her head. "No! Alard is...perhaps the only friend I have in town, that's all. Everyone else hates me, calling me a witch and saying I murdered my parents."

"You are a witch. Their witch." When Grandmother said it, it sounded like an honourable occupation, instead of an insult.

"No, that's you, Grandmother. You cure their ills. I just deliver things, and collect the payment."

Grandmother waved away her doubts. "I do

nothing that you cannot. And while my magic is waning, yours grows stronger every day. Why, with a wave of your hand, you could clear the whole village of tonight's snowfall. They'd pay attention to you then!"

"They'd still call me a witch, only louder," Rosa grumbled, before her grandmother's words sank in. "Wait...snow? It has not snowed here since the winter my parents died! That was the coldest winter in living memory, you said, the sort that we won't see again for a hundred years. It's only been six!"

"The weather does not count the years. It merely is. And I fear this winter will be colder than any we have yet known. I think we have waited long enough. The snow is a sign from the gods, that it is time I initiated a new priestess. Will you be ready for the Midwinter rites?"

With Grandmother's eyes reading her very soul, Rosa could not lie. "No. I had thought to ask Alard, but now...I cannot imagine any man in the village I would want to share the ceremony with."

Grandmother patted her hand. "If the gods

want you for their priestess, they will provide. Who knows? Perhaps the folktales your mother loved so much will come true, and a knight will come riding into town in pursuit of some noble quest. No man could fail to notice you."

Yes, notice her and label her a witch, his voice full of venom as he spat the words. Yet, "Yes, Grandmother," was all Rosa said.

"It's settled, then. At Midwinter, you will pledge yourself fully to the goddess, as her priestess. The snow will come, and we must guard against it as best we can." Grandmother clapped her hands. "Which is why I need new boots. You don't feel the cold as I do, but when you are my age, you'll know!"

Rosa nodded numbly. Snow brought the wolves down from the mountains. Perhaps she would have her chance at vengeance this winter. If she killed the wolf who'd killed her family, then the men of the village might look on her with admiration instead. She only needed one who was willing to worship the goddess...but she had little hope of even one as things stood now. Once she'd slayed the beast, though…

There was no doubt in her mind that she could kill the wolf. It was merely a matter of how, and when.

As an untrained girl, she'd sent the wolf running all those years ago. Now, with her magic completely under her command, he'd be no match for her.

# Eight

The village inn tempted Chase more than he liked to admit. He'd spent so many nights sleeping under hedges, as summer gave way to autumn and the infernal rain that never ceased, that the very thought of a night in a real bed, perhaps even a few hours seated before a fire, made his knees weak.

He counted his coins. He had enough for a hot meal or two and a bed, as long as it wasn't their best room. Abraham would have laughed at him, counting coppers like this. Then again, Abraham would have turned them to gold at a touch.

But Abraham was lost to him, and this was his life now. So Chase surrendered what remained of his wealth to the innkeeper and asked if the man knew of anyone in need of a knight.

The innkeeper scratched his head. "Don't know anyone who can afford to keep a knight, except for the king himself, and I'm sure he doesn't need any more. Not like we're at war with anyone right now. But if you're fixing to make a name for yourself so the king might hire you, you might try your hand at monster slaying."

"Monsters don't exist," Chase said.

The innkeeper's pitying look took him by surprise. "Then you're the only man who hasn't heard of the cursed wolf of the north, or the Kasmirus dragon."

Chase shook his head. "Indeed I haven't. Perhaps you could pour me an ale and tell me the story?"

"I'll do you one better. Go speak to the crier, sent out to search for a dragonslayer. He's seen the dragon himself." The innkeeper pointed at a boy not much younger than Chase, unrolling a scroll on the table.

Fighting a beast might be better than killing another man, enemy or no, Chase told himself. He'd seen enough death.

He turned his head to better read the boy's poster.

Heroes wanted, the poster read, for monster slaying of all kinds. Apply within.

Not that he was much of a hero, whatever the herald in Aros had said. Monster slaying might help him earn both his keep and a real reputation. It would at least keep his thoughts from straying to Abraham and Maja a dozen times a day.

Chase raised his voice. "Are you looking for a hero, boy?"

The boy looked up. He looked…resigned, Chase thought. As if to emphasise his point, the boy sighed.

Chase pulled the poster toward him. He tapped the crudely drawn dragon. "Where's the dragon and what's the reward?"

"Kasmirus, between the city and the river," the boy said. He didn't show a trace of fear.

Interesting. Either the beast wasn't so fearsome, or the boy hadn't actually seen it. "But I don't know the reward. Every time it kills another knight, the king increases it."

A dragon that could kill many knights was definitely fearsome.

"How big is the beast, and does it breathe fire?" Chase persisted.

Now the boy showed the first hint of fear, his Adam's apple bobbing as he swallowed nervously. "It would scarcely fit in the square outside, and its fiery breath is so hot, it has been known to melt a man's armour." He shuddered.

He'd seen this melting in person. Yet he'd survived. By running or hiding, or both, Chase decided. This boy was no dragon slayer.

A fire breathing monster who melted armour and had killed many knights. Such a beast would take a true hero to slay it – the sort of brave, foolhardy man who would undertake a quest for the sheer glory of it. Chase was too sensible a man for such things.

Chase lifted his hand and the scroll rolled up. "Which means it's impossible to kill."

He resolved to ask the innkeeper about the wolf. That wouldn't be an impossible task.

"Not impossible," the boy countered. "All creatures must die some time."

Chase stared at the boy. There was a steel to him, that his youth had hidden until now. The boy himself might not slay the dragon, but he was determined to recruit the man who could do the deed. Perhaps he'd known one of the slayed knights, a father or mentor, perhaps. He had a personal grudge against this dragon, but wasn't silly enough to fight it alone and die unmourned.

Chase grinned. "Even us. But there's nothing heroic about being roasted alive. I'm Sir Chase." He held out his hand.

"George," the boy said, clasping Chase's arm briefly before letting go.

Chase gestured to the innkeeper. "Two more ales for me and my friend here!" When the innkeeper nodded, Chase turned back to George. "Where are you headed?"

"Aros," George said.

Chase swallowed. From the maw of a fire breathing dragon to the court of Aros' icy queen? He had to warn him. "Not a good city for heroes, Aros," he managed to say. "Their queen isn't fond of adventurers." He suppressed a shudder as he took a cup of ale from the innkeeper.

George raised his eyebrows. "That's not what I heard. When they hold tourneys, the queen richly rewards the victor. She holds heroes in high regard, or so it is said." George drank deeply.

Sir Chase choked on his ale. Wiping his mouth with the back of his hand, he said, "Aye, I heard the same. Until I met the woman. Beautiful as the day is long, but cold as ice. Looking into her eyes is enough to freeze your soul, and no mistake."

He had a peculiar vision of Queen Margareta facing down a fire breathing dragon. It would be an even match, Chase thought.

Now, if it was that princess daughter of hers...the dragon would be doomed. But princesses did not fight dragons. Pity. He'd pay money to see a girl fight. Like Maja had wanted to, but their father had forbidden it. He'd like to see anyone try to refuse the princess of Aros, if she wanted to take up a sword.

"Then I'll be sure to avoid her," George said.

That wouldn't be hard. The boy wouldn't be invited to a feast where he might meet the princess.

"Wise choice." Chase raised his ale. "And I will avoid your dragon. I heard about a pack of troublesome wolves in the north. I might go see to those instead."

George clunked his cup against Chase's. "To both our good health, and long lives," he said gravely, and drank.

Without the interference of women, Chase added silently as he downed his ale. Women and wolves didn't mix, so he'd be safe in the north.

# Nine

"Now, will you be all right brewing all that up by yourself?" Grandmother asked, surveying the jars of honey that covered the table.

Rosa didn't spare the table a glance. "Of course. I'd sooner brew ten times this much than go into town again after yesterday."

Grandmother shook her head. "The townspeople will never show you the respect you deserve unless you believe you deserve it. You are their witch, soon to be their priestess, far more important than the Baron and his line, for our family has been here for centuries.

You must wear your magic boldly, with pride, much like your red cloak. But today, save your magic for your brewing, for that is how the best mead is made."

Rosa bowed her head. "Yes, Grandmother." There was no point in arguing – Grandmother had earned the respect of the villagers and the Baron, but Rosa knew she could never ignore the taunts when her own head told her they were right.

She might not have murdered her own family, but their blood lay on her hands. If she'd been home, her magic might have saved them, as it had saved herself.

But she'd arrived too late.

Grandmother's eyes brimmed with sympathy. "You dwell too much on the past and what cannot be changed, Rosa. Look up, to the future, for that is where hope lies."

Not until the wolf was dead, she thought but did not say. Instead, she managed a smile. "My future is all about boiling and brewing, until all the barrels are full of mead. Which I hope will taste as good as the last batch."

Grandmother returned her smile. "Better,

I'm sure. You've learned so much since last winter, the village will have no need of me any more." She swept her cloak around herself and strode out before Rosa could respond.

For a moment, Rosa was a lost little girl again, all alone with barely a breath of magic to call upon, before she took a deep breath and reminded herself that girl had grown up. Stronger, more powerful. Powerful enough to seek vengeance when the wolf returned, she hoped.

And strong enough to brew an ocean of medicinal mead alone.

She stoked the fire, filled the cauldron from the well, and set it on the fire to boil. Then she headed outside and lit the firepits, which would be blazing hot enough to heat the other cauldrons once she'd filled them.

Her day consisted of wood, water and watching for bubbles, stirring in the honey, setting the mixture aside to cool, before sealing it up in barrels to ferment for a few weeks.

Then she could use her magic to lift the barrels up to the loft, where the warmth from the winter fire would help the brew mature.

Darkness had fallen by the time she'd stopped stoking the fires, but she couldn't leave the cauldrons out in night's chill and let ice ruin her hard work. She filled the last few barrels and sent them soaring inside with their fellows.

Only then did she allow herself to head back into the house to rest. Too exhausted to cook, she swallowed a few bites of bread and cheese.

Rosa's arms ached as she brought in wood to feed the fire for the night, but her day's work would go to waste if she let the fire go out. Not to mention Grandmother would admonish her for such laziness when she returned in the morning, for surely Grandmother had accepted the Baron's hospitality for the night instead of walking home so late in the dark.

So Rosa toppled into bed and fell asleep almost instantly, without a worry in the world.

# *Ten*

Morning held an unfamiliar chill, forcing Rosa to reach for a shawl to wrap around her shoulders as she rekindled the fire from the coals. A cup of willow bark tea would see off the aches from yesterday's labour, before today's began.

Seeing as she'd left yesterday's milk in the cellar and forgotten about it, after today's milking, she might have enough to make cheese. She left a pot of water over the fire to boil, then headed outside to the barn where the goats slept.

Snow had turned their fertile, dark soil white. Rosa cursed, then summoned a whirlwind to whisk it away from Grandmother's garden. The spells Grandmother had cast on the clearing usually kept all but that hardiest frost away – she had an arrangement with the surrounding trees, or so she'd said – but perhaps even trees could not keep a snowstorm out completely.

No wonder Grandmother had stayed the night with the Baron. Walking through snow was…to return to trudging through despair, that winter Rosa had lost her family to the wolf. The coldest winter in living memory, or so everyone had said. She hadn't felt the cold, for she'd been too wrapped up in her grief. But now…snow sent a chill through her heart that had nothing to do with grief.

This year, her family would have justice. And snow would not touch her or hers again. Rosa bit her lip, strengthening the spell that swirled the snow away from her home so that it would not stop until the storm was over.

Better than dwelling on the evidence that Grandmother's magic was weakening.

A faint sound reached her ears, and Rosa sent a gust of wind to tell her more. The sound grew louder, until she could discern the crunch of wheels on the snow dusted road, accompanied by the low voices of the men who drove the wagon.

Milking and cheesemaking would have to wait. Rosa had time to comb her hair and straighten her cloak before the wagon trundled into view, accompanied by three guards and Alard.

Despite the freezing wind, all four of them removed their hats and held them to their chests.

Rosa's heart sank.

"Alard, what's happened?" she demanded, looking from him to the wagon and back again. Casks stood on either side of a covered lump that ran the length of the wagon. "What's all this?"

"Ah…this is my father's gift to you. And your grandmother. As thanks for all that you do for the village. All supplies from our cellar to help you through the winter. You'll need it, now that…"

"What, Alard?" Rosa couldn't keep the bite of impatience out of her tone.

One of Alard's men twitched the cloth aside. Beneath it was Grandmother's green cloak, ending in a pair of brand new boots.

"No!" Rosa doubled over. Not Grandmother. The only family she had left. "What happened?" she demanded.

"My father asked her to stay last night, but she refused. She insisted on walking home. One of the woodcutters found her this morning, lying in the snow on the road at the edge of the forest. Some cowardly creature had attacked her..."

Dread curled in Rosa's belly. There was only one creature it could have been.

Rosa reached for her grandmother's cloak, exposing the old woman's throat. Or what would have been her throat, if the wolf hadn't ripped it out.

"My father wanted to bury her in the churchyard, where our family lie, but I knew she wouldn't have wanted that. That you would want..." Alard couldn't seem to finish.

"Yes. She would want to be buried in the

woods, where she lived," Rosa lied. Alard and all the Baron's family worshipped the new religion, the one with the dying deity, instead of the multiple gods she knew lived in this part of the world. The gods her grandmother had prayed to and sacrificed to every day of her life. Grandmother would be accorded a funeral appropriate for a High Priestess who'd served the forest gods – her body would be burned on their altar, and her ashes scattered to strengthen the forest.

"My father has sent men out to hunt the creature, before it kills anyone else," Alard said. "You need not fear. I will bring you its head myself."

Rosa shook her head. "It's the wolf. The same one who killed my family. It came for her. Your hunters will not find it. It's too clever for that. When it comes, it will come for me. And I will be ready for it, this time. I will bring you its head. I'll carry it through the streets and maybe then, people will finally believe that it was a wolf, not me, who killed my family."

Alard looked alarmed. "We do believe you!

No one thinks such a terrible thing. But now that your grandmother is gone, perhaps you should consider moving to the village. I would be happy to offer you the hospitality of the Great House..." His eyes shone with eagerness.

"And who will placate the gods of the forest, with Grandmother gone? No, Alard, I will not move to town. I will stay here, where I belong." She eyed the wagon. "The supplies you brought should see me through the winter."

"But what then? I know your grandmother was a powerful witch, but you..." Oh, so earnest. Even when he insulted her.

Rosa bit down hard, tasting blood. "I am my grandmother's successor, and anyone who thinks my power is any less than hers is welcome to test it." She sent a gust of wind across the clearing, lifting Grandmother's cape from her body and making it dance as though her spirit animated the cloth, ten feet up in the air. The cloak reached the space between the firepits, and Rosa felt the faint warm air current stirring from the not-quite-dead coals.

She sent the breeze swirling through the coals, four gouts of flame that climbed higher than her house. "But not before I have sought justice for my family." She swallowed. "And Grandmother." Tears threatened, but she blinked them away. She would not cry in front of these men.

"Rosa…"

She ignored Alard. "You may store the supplies in the cellar. I'm sure if I must take up my grandmother's healing duties on top of my own, I won't have time to do it. But if your families have need of healing throughout the winter, be assured your kindness will be remembered."

Alard's men nodded and set about unloading the wagon.

Rosa let the air lift Grandmother's body, carrying it to where her cloak lay spread out on the ground, between the firepits. She gently laid the body down, like a queen lying in state. For to the forest, Grandmother had been the queen of the trees.

A power Rosa did not share, though they'd both been able to practice a small amount of healing. Rosa would have to work harder on the herb garden now, without Grandmother's magic to make it flourish.

The men carried casks, jars and sacks into the house. Rosa took stock of it all, stashing the information into a corner of her mind for later, when she could think about such things.

"There's space in the wagon for your things. Please come back to the village, so we can keep you safe. Just for the winter, until the wolf is caught," Alard wheedled.

"My place is here," Rosa said, planting her feet. She looked the Baron's son in the eye. "That wolf will die by winter's end, Alard."

He nodded once. "Yes, it will."

# Eleven

The town looked no different to any of the
others Chase had travelled through to get here.
The only difference was the depth of the snow,
which had fallen steadily until even his mare
struggled through the drifts. What passed for a
Great House here – the seat of the local baron,
he'd been told – looked like one of the bigger
outbuildings on Abraham's estate. A stone
barn, not a castle.

But he didn't have the time or funds to be
choosy. Winter was well and truly here, and his
need for shelter at night had forced him to sell

his armour, piece by piece, until nothing remained. If this town wasn't the one beset by wolves, he might have to sell his horse to make it through the winter.

No, fate would not be so cruel. She might not want him to live comfortably in the service of the royal court of Aros, but fate could not be such a bitch that she wanted him to die in a ditch halfway to nowhere. But fate was a woman, and a traitorous one at that. He wanted nothing to do with women when his business was with wolves.

He headed for the Great House, leading his exhausted mare.

"You're not from around here."

The voice came out of nowhere, until the owner appeared from behind what Chase had thought was a snowdrift. Now, he saw it was a half-buried building. A woodshed, judging by the pile of wood in the man's arms.

Chase stopped. "No, I'm not. My name is Sir Chase, and I heard your town had a wolf problem. I've come to take care of it." He hoped, he thought but didn't say.

Logs tumbled from the man's arms into the

snow. "Master Alard will be pleased to hear it." He headed for the house, and opened the door. "Boy, fetch Master Alard! A knight has come to slay the wolf!"

Chase heard the sound of running feet before the man closed the door again.

The man stuck out his hand. "I'm Wido. My family have served the Baron's for generations. But we've never had a wolf this bad. First six years ago, in that cold winter, and we thought it'd gone, but it's back, and more murderous than ever. Last time it murdered a whole family in their house as they slept!"

Chase's heart sank. That didn't sound like a wolf at all. What had he gotten himself into?

But it was too late now. He had no money left. If he did not take this job, he would starve before spring.

"Sir Knight, our saviour!" A well-dressed man of about Chase's own age appeared, his arms held wide as if he intended to embrace him. He did, kissing Chase on both cheeks. "I'm Alard. I thought we wouldn't see anyone else until the spring, though I sent riders out in every direction. Angels must have sent you!"

"An innkeeper on the road between Aros and Kasmirus, actually," Chase said.

Alard's eyes widened. "And you chose to help us instead of slaying the dragon? We are blessed indeed!"

The admiration in the man's eyes made Chase feel uncomfortable. "Hold your praise until the job is done, Baron Alard."

Alard shook his head. "My father is the Baron. I'm just Alard, for as long as my father lives. Which I hope will be a long time."

Chase could detect no lie in the man's fierce words. Perhaps Alard truly was a loving son, who had no desire to rule his father's lands. "I'm Sir Chase."

Alard's eyes shone. "Well met, Sir Chase. Tell me what you need to end this plague, and it shall be yours."

"Plague? I thought your problem was a wolf!" A wolf was one thing, but the plague was enough to send him galloping as far and fast as his mare could take him, winter snows be damned.

"The wolf that plagues us, yes. God forbid any other misfortunes befall us this winter!"

Chase breathed out a sigh of relief. "I heard there was a bag of gold on offer as reward for anyone who slays the beast."

Alard nodded. "Yes, that is so."

Chase took a deep breath. "I must ask for more than that. Board and lodging until spring, which are mine no matter how long it takes me to exterminate your wolf. Whether it takes me a week or the rest of the winter. I have travelled far, and – "

"Of course! You shall have a bed in my father's house, and a seat at his table for as long as you like. Rid us of this wolf, and my father may never want you to leave!" Alard clapped his hands. "You there – take Sir Chase's horse and see it is well cared for. Have his things brought to the house."

A man took the reins from Chase and led the mare to the stables.

"Now, join me for dinner. We'll broach a barrel of my father's best wine, and you can tell us tales of other monsters you have slain!" Alard said, gesturing for Chase to follow him.

No matter what the man had done, Abraham was no monster, and Chase had not slain him. "Better that you tell me more about this wolf. Now I am here, I am eager to start. Perhaps even on the morrow."

Alard nodded agreeably. "Of course, of course! You are a true hero, Sir Chase, to be so intent on your quest! I shall tell you everything I know."

And as the words spilled out of the Baron's son, Chase began to have an inkling of a plan. Wolves were crafty beasts, and one who sneaked into a house to kill people as they slept was craftier still. Waiting for it to appear and maybe kill again would never do. But if he could lure it into a trap, where he lay in wait with his bow, he might be able to accomplish this after all.

# Twelve

Rosa could delay no longer. The ashes from her grandmother's pyre were cold on the stone altar in the forest, and she had made more cheese than she could eat in a year. The mead would not finish fermenting for some days yet, and Alard's hunters had followed the wolf's trail to a clearing in the forest, before they'd lost it.

Treating the hunters' coughs and chills from sleeping in the snow had given her all the information she needed to head out on her own hunt, along with the certainty that no one else would be out in the forest, risking his neck against the beast. The Baron's hunters didn't dare cross the witch who was now the town's only healer, who'd ordered them to rest inside for a week.

She'd sacrificed four elderly hens to use as bait, or she intended to – the old broilers were still alive, stuffed in the sack over her shoulder. Fresh blood mattered to predators, and surely this wolf was no different.

She found the clearing easily enough, though there were no wolf prints to be seen with the fresh dusting of snow the ground had received since the hunters had last been here. But it mattered not. She had no intention of tracking the beast to its lair. Instead, she intended to lure it out with the smell of fresh meat.

Rosa moved to the middle of the clearing to slaughter the chickens. Her experienced hands made quick work of the killing part, but she took her time gutting the carcasses, throwing entrails across the snow to spread the blood further.

When she was satisfied that she'd made

enough of a mess, she washed her hands and sought a suitable vantage point from which she could see clearly while she waited for dusk. The tallest tree was not the stoutest, but she was light enough to make the climb, if she kept close to the trunk. She climbed as high as she dared, before unwrapping the coil of rope she'd worn around her waist to tie herself securely to the trunk.

Only then did she string her bow, knowing speed would be her ally once the wolf appeared. The more arrows she could sink into its hide, the better chance she had of killing it before morning. Then perhaps the souls of her family would let her sleep without nightmares.

Wrapping her cloak tightly around her to keep out the cold, Rosa settled down to wait.

She must have fallen into a light doze, for she opened her eyes to darkness, or near enough. The full moon above lit the clearing, turning the reddened snow into the black of corruption. And yet…something moved across it, like a cloud, but more corporeal.

She plucked an arrow from her quiver and nocked it, ready to fire. The creature moved closer to the chickens, and Rosa loosed.

The arrow found its mark, but the creature that collapsed on the snow was too small to be the wolf. Its tail twitched once, then was still. A silvery fox, she thought, drawn by the bait. Not the wolf at all.

She slumped against the tree. Well, the fox would now be bait, too. She considered going down to retrieve her arrow and perhaps butcher the fox, to spread more fresh blood over the scene, but decided not to bother. She had plenty of arrows, and all night to wait.

Silence descended on the clearing again. Rosa longed for a hot meal, or even a flask of mead, but she hadn't thought to bring more than a chunk of ham, as she was already heartily sick of cheese.

Mead would have ruined her aim, anyhow, she told herself as she munched on the cold ham.

Something slammed into the trunk of her tree, nearly shaking her out of it, and the ham fell from her fingers to the ground below.

A second passed, and she heard the sound of chewing, accompanied by a faint whine, like a dog in pain.

Whatever it was crashed into the tree a second time. Then a third.

Rosa hung on for dear life, hoping the rope around the trunk would hold.

Then she heard the sound of scrabbling, like the creature was digging a hole in the snow.

Or a grave.

Rosa shook herself. Animals did not dig graves.

The sounds stopped, but she barely had a moment to breathe a sigh of relief before something hit the tree, harder than before. Again. And again.

On the fourth blow, the tree tipped sideways at an alarming angle, spilling Rosa off her branch into space. Only the rope around her kept her from falling.

The tree shuddered from the force of another blow, and the rope became uncomfortably tight. She flung her arms out to catch anything that might support her weight, but she dangled too far away to touch anything.

Cursing, Rosa pulled out her knife and

began sawing at the rope as another blow sent the tree toppling against the one beside it. A smaller tree that began to buckle under the weight...

Rosa sawed faster, barely noticing as she scraped her fingers raw on the rope, for her attention was directed down, in the hope that the snowdrift below would be deep enough to break her fall.

But all she could see was a pair of glowing blue eyes, staring straight at her.

The wolf, she knew without a doubt.

The beast flung itself at the tree trunk again.

Ominous cracks sounded, though whether from her tree or the other, Rosa couldn't be sure.

She could feel the rope stretching, unravelling, ready to drop her within reach of the waiting wolf, but her blood-slicked fingers hummed with power. The rope snapped, but the air caught her, as she had commanded it to. She spread her cloak, letting the wind carry her to the lower branches of the next tree.

A much sturdier tree than her first choice, though she could no longer see much of the clearing.

The wolf's eyes followed her, as if the creature could see her.

No, surely not. Wolves saw movement, and used scent to find their prey. If she stayed still against the trunk, it would lose interest in her and investigate the chickens instead.

The wolf that had let the fox go first, like some sort of scout, before attacking the very tree she sat in. Where the arrow had come from...

No. Wolves were not that clever. Men thought like that, ones skilled in battle. Not animals.

Something closed on her boot. Rosa kicked out, and was rewarded with a whine as the wolf let go. She scrambled higher up the tree, out of reach.

Why wouldn't it leave her alone? Surely now it would go and eat...

But the wolf sat down in a patch of moonlight, turning those glowing eyes up at her as if to say it could wait all night.

It could, she realised. It could wait all night and all day, its fur protecting it from the cold.

Whereas she had no food, not enough rope to secure herself, and she'd have to sleep sometime. When she did...she'd fall, and the wolf would have her.

No. If she had to climb a hundred trees and ride the air currents until dawn, the wolf would not touch her. If the creature really was a wolf, which she was beginning to doubt.

She began to climb.

# Thirteen

It hadn't been a hundred trees, but she had lost count after the first dozen. She'd climbed until she could not reach any higher, then summoned a gust of wind to carry her across the treetops to another tree, which she would climb to the highest point before doing the same again.

She fell more than she flew, letting the spread cloak slow her descent, but as the night went on, her mind considered how she might improve upon her situation. Something larger and more rigid than her cloak to catch the air, big enough to lie upon full-length as it buoyed her up. But not too heavy, for the air could only lift so much.

Rosa reached for the next tree, willing herself to climb it with her aching arms, even if the wolf was no longer in sight. Until the sun rose, she knew the hunter would not sleep.

How did she know that?

Rosa turned it over in her mind, until she found the answer. Magic. Whatever had turned that creature into what it was now, it was magical. A cursed king, an enchanted wolf…what difference did it make? It was no woodland creature to fall into an ordinary trap like the fox had.

No, the creature had a man's cunning.

A man who wanted to kill her.

Who had already killed her family.

A creature that would be the next to die.

Not her.

But she would need a new plan, now she knew what she was hunting.

Dawn took her by surprise, as she reached the top of a tree that wasn't far from her cottage. She could see the stone altar below, still dusted in ash.

Grandmother, I will avenge you, she swore as she summoned a final gust to take her safely to the forest floor.

Her legs felt as soft as ricotta when she landed, but Rosa didn't dare stay here. She could not rest until the stout walls of the cottage kept the wolf out.

With a brief thanks to the gods of the wood for the gift of her magic and for delivering her home safely, she trudged toward the cottage.

Only to find that despite all her efforts, someone had beaten her home anyway.

# Fourteen

Deep in his cups, Alard had grasped Chase's arm with both hands. "Promise me something, Sir Chase," he'd slurred.

Chase had nodded once, encouraging the man to continue.

"Warn the witch. She lives in a cottage in the woods. Tell her you're here at my request to slay the wolf. Tell her to stay out of the woods, where she'll be safe."

Chase had nodded again, agreeing to the man's request. What else could he say, anyway?

"Thank you," Alard had breathed, before

pitching face-first onto the table and starting to snore.

Chase had reclaimed his arm and headed off to his own bed, where he'd slept like the dead.

Now, dawn found him outside in the cold, packing enough food into his saddlebags for a week-long hunt while one of the stable boys fetched him several extra quivers of arrows from the armoury. It had been a long time since he'd last hunted with Abraham, and he missed the man more than ever. A few jokes would make his grim task so much easier, but it was not to be.

Alard and the Baron were still in their beds, as Chase would be, too, if he'd been in the Rumpelstiltskin Castle with Maja and Abraham. Or even if he'd stayed at the court in Aros.

Chase shook himself. He could no longer live in the past. He had a wolf to kill, and a new life to make. A life of his own, without Maja or Abraham or the help of some far-off court.

But first he had to find a witch, a woman who worked magic like the curse that had turned Abraham from a sane man into a mad one.

He set off into the woods, glad to find the snow lay light on the ground under the trees, unlike in town. The path was well-worn, too, as if many villagers travelled to see the witch. He wondered what the village priest would say about such things. Chase could not recall seeing a church in town, come to think of it. His father would certainly turn over in his grave if he knew.

But here, so far from civilisation, it was easy to see that the old ways would not die easily. Especially without a church to remind the people that they were supposed to believe in a new faith now.

While living in a world with numerous gods and monsters, curses and magic. Chase shivered as the town vanished from sight between the trees.

His horse felt no such chill, as she plodded onward.

He must be imagining the dread that coursed through him, he decided. He struck up a bawdy tune, and sang at the top of his lungs to pass the time.

He'd managed to sing it through three times, or at least the verses he remembered, before the cottage came into view. Stone walls topped with thick thatch, which bore only a light dusting of snow. A small enclosure beside it held two goats, several chickens and a stable of sorts, with a carefully laid out garden in the space between. Even in the dead of winter, the garden showed signs of life, for the snow had not completely covered it yet.

Magic, the sneaky voice in the back of his mind told him, but he hushed it. It was nothing of the sort. The surrounding trees evidently kept this place clear of snow, much like they'd protected the road to reach here.

And there was the witch, crossing the clearing to reach her door, her white hair coming loose from her braid.

Chase's heart relaxed. An old, wise woman – no wonder Alard wanted her warned and protected. Her knowledge of healing herbs was surely important to his people.

Chase stepped out of the shadows, straightening his shoulders to make himself look more heroic than he felt. "Fear not, mistress. Your Baron has sent me to slay the wolf. If you but keep to your cottage, I will soon make the forest safe for a gentle woman such as yourself."

The witch whirled, sending her cloak flying out around her in a swirl of blood, for it was as red as the stuff in his veins. "Then the Baron is a fool, for who will make the forest safe for the likes of you?"

Chase's mouth dropped open, and he could not seem to close it. What he'd taken for an old woman was nothing of the sort.

Her youthful face and equally youthful figure – for her thick woollen dress only emphasised the curve of the flesh beneath it – were nothing to the blue fire in her eyes that held him transfixed.

Then she smiled, just a little, and Chase's heart turned to mush.

"Go. Find something else to slay. A dragon, or some such thing. There is magic at work here that you cannot begin to understand." She flicked her fingers in dismissal.

That flick broke the spell, somehow, and

Chase's tongue unfroze. "I cannot simply leave," he said stiffly. "I have accepted a quest, and it would be dishonourable to run away before it is complete. I am a knight, and my honour is more precious than my own life. I would not expect a woman to understand matters of honour."

Her smile widened to a grin. "Then you're a bigger fool than the Baron, Sir Knight. Honour is about doing what's right, and the right thing for you to do is leave this forest. Now. While you still have your life." She opened the door of her cottage, stepped inside, then slammed it shut.

Chase opened his mouth to defend himself, but that would be pointless – she wouldn't hear a word of it. And what could he say to convince her she was wrong?

Nothing.

Deeds spoke louder than words.

So he would let his deeds speak for him. He would kill this wolf, drop its head on her doorstep, and then she'd see who was a fool. He nudged his horse to continue along the path, in the direction the witch had come from.

That wolf would die before the day was done, he swore.

# Fifteen

More than anything, Rosa wanted to sleep, but sleep refused to come. Her grandmother's words haunted her – she had predicted the arrival of a knight, right in time for Midwinter. A pity she hadn't predicted the wolf, too.

If that poor fool of a knight did not take her advice and instead went hunting for the wolf…it was his body she'd find next.

She told herself she didn't care what happened to a stranger. Men could do whatever foolish things they pleased in the forest, and if it got them killed…

But it was her job to protect those who wandered into the forest. She served the gods of the forest, as her grandmother and all the witches before her had, and this was her domain.

Especially when there was magic involved.

For no one else in the village or any of the towns around was a witch.

And to serve the gods of the forest properly, to become their priestess instead of just a novice, she needed that knight. Alive.

Cursing, she rose from her bed and opened the door to see if the knight still waited outside.

To her surprise, he seemed to have taken her advice and headed back to town, for there was no sign of him or his horse.

Good.

She longed to go back inside, but her conscience would not allow it. For if the Baron had sent one fool into the woods, he would send more. And she might not be able to warn them all.

With one last, longing look at her bed, she fastened her cloak and set out for the village.

The boys who had taunted her before her grandmother's death were engaged in a snowball fight in the snowdrift beside the road, too busy to pay attention to her.

Or so Rosa thought, until a snowball came sailing her way.

Did the little brats know she'd spent all night in the forest, protecting them? Risking her life for theirs? They would never have dared to throw such a thing at her grandmother.

Magic came to her as easily as breathing now. A puff of air turned the snowball into a flurry that swirled harmlessly to the road at her feet.

She turned to face the boys. "Next time, that's what will happen to you," she said.

The boys' eyes widened in horror before they bolted.

She shook her head at the gullibility of small boys. As if she could summon a wind strong enough to do such a thing. The worst she could do to them was lift them onto their parents' roof or into a nearby tree, and they'd probably just climb down in any case.

Rosa felt eyes upon her as she approached the Great House. Before her grandmother's death, she would have tried to ignore the prickle between her shoulder blades and the person causing it, but today she was done with evasions.

She would turn and face the wolf, if that's what it was, and anyone else presented so little threat compared to the dread beast that she feared no one.

"Is there a leaf clinging to my cloak, that you stare so?" she snapped.

"You do not deserve something so fine. Not when you scarcely give him the time of day. It should have been mine," a female voice hissed.

Piroska sat outside the smithy where her father worked, her eyes burning hotter than the forge.

The silly girl thought Alard had given her this cloak? Ah, the girl's jealousy had made her foolish indeed. Especially when Rosa was certain the cloak had been a gift from the Baron to Grandmother, like many of the valuable items in the cottage. Except for the beautiful woven carpet hidden in the loft.

Grandmother had blushed like a maiden when she'd described the Crusader knight who'd given her that particular item.

Rosa had always thought there was more to that story than her grandmother had said, and now it was too late to ask. She would never know.

"Have you ever asked him for a new cloak? After all you give him, seeing as he won't even let you keep his child, surely he owes you something," Rosa said.

Two spots of red appeared on Piroska's cheeks as her hand flew to her belly. "I'm sure I have no idea what you mean."

As if Rosa had read the girl's thoughts, she knew Piroska hadn't taken the latest elixir yet, or Alard had not yet given it to her. She still carried Alard's baby.

Rosa smiled. "In a village as small as this, nothing remains a secret long from the village witch. Least of all about the girl who might one day become the next baroness."

"I'd be a better one than you!" Piroska spat.

The girl was right, but Rosa did not need to tell her that. The next baroness would need to be a brood mare, or the Baron's bloodline would die out and the king would give these lands to someone else. Someone who might not respect the gods of the forest as much as the Baron and his ancestors.

Yet another thing to confront Alard about: wolves, and now his choice of wife. If Grandmother were here…but she wasn't, so this task fell to her now, too.

Being the next baroness, to be endlessly bedded by Alard in between popping out babies, would be such an easy life compared to being the village witch. But Rosa would still be expected to waddle around the village in between births. Better that Piroska bear the babies. Or any girl, really.

Alard might one day be the Baron, but he was a bore in bed. Or was that a boor?

Not the sort of passion suitable for a priestess, anyway.

Rosa walked on, into the main hall of the Great House.

"Alard!" she shouted.

"Ngh?" A man lifted his head from the table on the dais. Had Alard been sleeping on it?

Rosa strode forward. "Alard?" She had never seen him look quite this dishevelled. Why, he looked like he needed to shave, after sleeping there all night. And here she thought he simply hadn't been old enough to grow a beard yet.

He beamed. "You came! I shall have the servants prepare a chamber for you at once. My mother's has not been used since – "

Rosa silenced him with a look. "I came to ask you why there was a knight on my doorstep this morning. A knight who believed he was on a quest to slay my wolf, Alard. Do you have any idea how dangerous that creature is?"

Alard yawned. "Of course, of course. It's a wolf that killed your family. Very dangerous indeed. Which, I'm sure, is why you are here. Accepting my invitation. I shall send someone to the next town for the priest at once, for the sooner we are married – "

"We're not getting married."

He stared at her. "Why, of course we are! Don't you remember that Midsummer when we sneaked away from the feast and lay together? We promised we would never part! I admit I should have taken you as my wife then, but Father was fine then. Now, there must be no delay."

Rosa screwed up her face. "Midsummer, six years ago? The first summer after I lost my family, and went to live with my grandmother? I was sixteen, Alard, and we'd both drunk too much mead. I'm surprised you remember anything of that night." She'd plied him with that much mead in the hope that he hadn't.

She had not been so drunk when she'd accepted the comfort his body offered. Those who had taken up the new religion believed such relations between a man and a woman to be a sin, but Rosa knew the gods of the forest thought otherwise. They expected their priestesses to encourage as much spilling of seed as possible, especially at their most sacred festivals. Particularly when a priestess in training began her novitiate, as she had that night.

Alard's kisses and caresses that night had been reverent to the point of goddess worship, which is why she had chosen him to share her mead in the moonlight before he helped her shed her virgin's blood before the altar.

One night of pleasure, consecrating her body to the fertility of the forest, before taking the bitter elixir at dawn to ensure no baby was born of the union.

"I dream of it every night, praying for you to share my bed again. There is no one else, Rosa. No one but you." He sounded so earnest, as if he truly believed his own words.

"What about Piroska?" she demanded.

"Piroska?" His face went blank. "You mean the blacksmith's daughter?"

"The same girl you asked me to mix an elixir for?" Rosa prompted.

Alard flushed. "That was nothing. I was merely doing the girl a favour. She had evidently done something untoward with some peasant boy or other and was too frightened to ask you herself, so she confided in me, begging for my help."

"Alard, half the town can hear you scream each other's names when you're rolling around in the hayloft together. Her father might be the only man who doesn't know, if only because of the noise in the smithy." She blew out a breath. "But I didn't come to talk about you and your...exploits. I came to talk about the knight, and the wolf."

Alard rose and seized her hands. "But we must. You must, Rosa. For my father...he is...he is not well, and I fear he has not long left."

"The Baron is ill?" She'd never known the man to have so much as a head cold. Grandmother had prided herself on the Baron's good health, and received many gifts from the man in thanks for it.

"After the shock of your grandmother's death, he took to his bed, and has hardly been out of it since, except last night, where he insisted on greeting the knight. I fear he already regrets it..." Alard led the way upstairs, to the private chambers.

Rosa half expected Alard to show her his mother's rooms first, but his worry for his father had driven any amorous or matrimonial matters out of his head.

"Mistress Rosa is here, Father," Alard said softly, gesturing for Rosa to precede him.

Mistress Rosa? She'd never been called that before.

Perhaps she had slept, after all, and this was a dream.

Except…in no dream, nightmare or otherwise, had she ever thought to see the Baron looking less alive than her grandmother's corpse. His skin had taken a grey cast, and no one was more surprised than Rosa when his eyes blinked open – he was not yet dead.

"Leave us, boy. See that you send the girl home with a gift befitting Mistress Saskia."

Alard frowned. "But, Father, Mistress Saskia is – "

"Always asking for more honey, to make mead. See that she has all that we have left." The Baron fixed his eyes on his son.

Alard bowed his head. "Yes, Father." He departed.

Baron Arnold turned his eyes on Rosa. "Do you have Saskia's gift for healing?"

She'd thought she had, but if her grandmother's healing magic had kept death at bay for who knew how long, Rosa didn't think she could match that kind of power. Yet she was the only witch he had, so she lifted her chin and said, "She said my magic was more powerful than hers, but I must assess your condition before I can say if I can help you."

She laid her hand on his forehead, bit her lip and closed her eyes, letting her magic sweep through his body. It reminded her of a weed-choked field, with some sort of strange growth pushing out the normal parts inside his body. In order to heal an affliction like this, she would need Grandmother's knowledge of plants and growth and her affinity with such things. Rosa could cure a cold or heal an infected wound, if she simply swept the foreign matter out of the blood the way she sent a gust of wind to do her bidding, but this...stuff...grew everywhere. Was a part of him.

Rosa released the Baron. She wanted to look anywhere but into his eyes, and yet she could look nowhere else. "What did my grandmother tell you about your condition?" she asked finally.

"That it is like a forest growing around a

castle. The walls will only remain strong for so long, but the forest will always win, in the end," he said.

Rosa nodded. "My grandmother kept the forest at bay. But now…" She didn't want to continue, for if the Baron didn't know about her grandmother's death…

"Now Saskia is gone, there is no one strong enough to fight it," the Baron finished for her. "Don't try to lie to a dying man, Mistress Rosa. As Saskia often told me, it is a witch's duty to tell the truth, however unpalatable it may be, for it will out in the end. Are you indeed a witch?"

Rosa nodded. "Of course, but my power is over air, not plants."

"Did your grandmother teach you the old ways? The ways of the forest?"

She nodded again. "She did."

"Then will you protect the village from the forest? You will take her place as priestess, when my son takes my place?"

She straightened her shoulders. "I took up my duties upon my grandmother's death, though I was helping her long before then. I do my duty not for you, or for the village, but for – "

"Hush. Saskia chose her successor well, I am sure. I never expected to outlive her, but she would not let me die, either. Even though the weeds within me grow stronger every day, she kept pushing them back. Refused to stay the night here, insisting she had to get back, to prepare you to be her replacement. If I regret anything, 'tis letting that good woman go. But I could not have held her against her will. Not Saskia."

"You are not responsible for the wolf," Rosa said. She was. And she would not shirk her responsibilities. Not in this.

"No, but I could have ordered the hunt earlier, when she urged me to, after your family was killed. Yet I did not, for we could ill spare the men. And there were no other attacks, so there was no need. Until now."

"I will not let the beast take another victim," Rosa said.

"Let the men kill it. My son boasts of a brave knight who will head them. A hero of many battles. Let the men do the work, for what else are we men for? But you...see that her spirit is appeased. When they bring that beast's body to lay it at your feet, see that it burns. For Saskia."

It might be a witch's duty to tell the truth, but Rosa could leave parts out. "When it is dead, I will see that the body burns," she said.

The Baron smiled faintly. "You are just like her. A witch, and a warrior. Make sure my son sees you safely home to your cottage with whatever he found in the cellar."

The Baron lay back against his pillows and closed his eyes. He began to snore.

Rosa took one last look at the man – for he would not live much longer, and she might not see him again – before she headed back downstairs.

Alard was waiting for her in the yard, supervising as a wagon was filled with things for her.

"I'm sorry, Alard," she said before he could ask. "At most, I can give you some medicine that will ease his pain. But there is little more I can do for him now."

He nodded. "Tell my men what you need,

and they will bring it back for you. You must stay here, to tend to him. To help him live as long as he can. I shall have rooms prepared – "

"NO!" It came out louder than Rosa expected, startling her, but everyone in the yard stopped to stare. "Alard, I will not stay here, as your wife or your kept healer. I am going home, right after I give your cook instructions so that she may prepare what is necessary to make your father comfortable in his remaining days. Nothing I can do will save your father, but if I do not hunt down that wolf, he may kill again. And I will not have that blood on my hands."

"Why do you persist in this ridiculous notion that you and only you can kill this beast? It is not a task for a girl. We have a knight, a true hero, who will do the deed. Let him be your champion. My father needs you. I need you."

She refused to be swayed by his wheedling tone.

"Either your knight will not find the beast, or he will be killed. He won't last the week, Alard."

His eyes lit up. "Then that is what I ask. A week. Stay here, safe, for a week. If the knight returns with the dead beast, as I expect, then you can go home, knowing you will be safe."

It would take her a week to work out how to outsmart the beast, but she would not spend it here. Not to mention Midwinter was less than a week away. "What will you give me in exchange for doing as you ask?"

Alard spread his arms wide, taking in the rapidly filling wagon and the men carrying more casks up from the cellars. "Anything you wish."

Rosa wet her lips. "Send for that priest. When he arrives, you will wed – "

"Thank God!"

Rosa continued, "You will wed Piroska, and do your utmost to beget an heir. For your father will rest more peacefully if he knows his bloodline will continue after you."

"Piroska? But – "

She gazed steadily back into his hurt eyes. "Forget Midsummer, and any childish passion you may have held for me. In a few days, you will become Baron, and the sooner you have an heir, the better. For that, you need a fertile wife. Fate has given you Piroska, and you would be a fool not to accept such a gift."

His voice came out hoarse. "If I agree to marry the girl, will you promise to stay safe?"

"A week, then, I agree to. A week where you may find me at home. For all the wolf attacks have been here in the village, but the beast would not dare come to the cottage." Truth, for there was ancient magic in the stones beneath it. Magic Alard did not need to know about.

Alard blew out a breath. He didn't look happy, but he said, "Very well. I shall send for the priest. But if you change your mind…"

"I won't." She wet her lips. "But warn your heroic knight that I think the beast has magic of some sort. The creature is not what it appears to be."

"Sir Chase needs no warnings. He set out early this morning with everything he needs. He swore to kill the beast, and I believe him. Have faith, Rosa."

The knight had not come back? That meant the poor fool was alone in the forest…beset by a beast he couldn't kill.

And she'd just given her word she wouldn't hunt the wolf for another week.

Cursing, she set off for home.

# Sixteen

As Chase headed steadily uphill, the trees thinned, until he came upon another clearing – but this one was covered in snow. Well, mostly snow. In the middle of it was the remains of what looked like a recent kill, ringed round with feathers and bloody wolf prints.

He surveyed the trees around the edge of the clearing and nodded in satisfaction. This was the place to set up his trap. All he needed was bait.

Movement at the top of the slope caught his eye – a rabbit, tugging at a scrap of grass that grew sideways out of the vertical cliff face. Chase strung his bow, then fitted an arrow to the bowstring. Without his golden armour, he wouldn't miss this time.

He exhaled, then released, knowing the arrow would hit its mark.

The rabbit didn't make a sound as it toppled over, dead.

Chase tied his mare to a trunk just inside the treeline, before scrambling up the slope to collect his kill. The best place to set the trap was…right here, he decided, pulling out a knife. He gutted the dead rabbit, flinging its entrails across the snow, before dropping the carcass among the mess. If that didn't attract the wolf, he didn't know what would.

Now all he had to do was climb a tree, and wait for the wolf to show up.

He'd shoot it, bring it back to the witch, then drag the carcass into town to collect his reward. Easy.

Chase settled into a suitable perch, wrapped his cloak around him, set his bow across his lap in readiness, and waited.

# Seventeen

By the time she'd reached home, Rosa still had no more idea of how better to slay the wolf than she had that morning, but she had thought up a plan of how to find the knight without breaking her word to Alard.

But in order for her plan to work, she needed to learn to fly before dusk, when the wolf would come out to hunt.

Rosa already knew her cloak wasn't good enough to achieve true flight. She needed something like a boat or a raft that could float on air. If her father, a carpenter, were still alive, he'd build something in moments, but she was not as practiced as he'd been with wood or tools. There had been an old door in the lumber pile, though…

She dug it out and laid it on the ground. All she had to do was fly it around the clearing. Rosa took a deep breath and bit her lip.

The door rose off the ground, but the higher she lifted it, the more magic it took, and she'd barely moved it yet. Sweat broke out on her forehead as she gave the hovering door a push. It toppled end over end before it righted itself, flying on a slight angle, before it tipped again, hanging sideways for a moment, before it plummeted.

Finally, she let it fall to earth. She could never travel atop the door if she couldn't hold it steady. Something lighter, perhaps.

A blanket flapped around the clearing with little effort, but when she tried to keep it steady, she found it impossible. The blanket rolled and folded with the slightest change of direction.

A woven screen her grandmother had sometimes placed before the fire to hide its light at night fared better, but air whistled through the gaps, so it lost height quickly, though it held steady.

The blanket pegged to the screen made its wobbly way around the clearing without falling, but the combination was almost as heavy as the door. Rosa could not fly across the forest on such a heavy raft.

Ready to give up, she carried the items back inside. It was getting late. She should start dinner soon. The knight would have to wait until the morrow, and survive on his wits for the night, such as they were.

Rosa decided to bring a smoked sausage down from the loft, and make a stew with it and some vegetables from the cellar. With the loft so full of fermenting mead barrels, she had to climb on top of them to reach the sausage. From her perch, she spotted her grandmother's prized Crusader carpet.

Thickly woven, with stiff backing, it might hold up for a flight...

She forgot the sausage and dragged the carpet outside, then spread it on the ground. If this didn't work, then she truly would give up for the day. But if it did…she would go and get the knight before dinner.

The surface undulated a little as it rose, but the carpet held steady, much like the screen. Rosa sent it around the clearing, lifting it higher as it went. The carpet did not weigh nearly as much as the screen or the door, and while it rippled a little, it did not roll up altogether, as the blanket had. She made it fly around the clearing a second time, level with the tree tops. As smooth as a bird in flight – once it had the air beneath it, it glided almost effortlessly.

Rosa laughed. What would her grandmother have said, watching her precious carpet flying about?

She would have said it was a waste of magic. What the carpet needed was a load to carry, or a passenger.

Her grandmother might have given the carpet a sack of vegetables to carry, but lack of sleep and her need to save the knight made her reckless. If she fell, she could slow her descent, she reasoned, as she swooped the carpet close enough for her to leap on.

She flung herself headlong at the carpet, clutching the edges in her desperation to stay on as she remembered to keep the air flowing beneath it, buoying her up.

She made the carpet do a slow lap around the clearing, close enough to the ground that a fall would not hurt her. Then she lifted it higher, letting it move faster. She did not understand it, but that seemed to take less magic.

Higher, then faster. The air obeyed her thought before she'd fully considered it, flying her almost to the treetops like a circling eagle.

Rosa's breath caught in her throat, her hair blowing back in the wind that seemed to claw at her eyes, but still she held on. By all that was holy, she was flying!

She let out a whoop of triumph and pushed the carpet higher, so it cleared the treetops altogether. The mountains rose up in the distance, snowy crags that gave way to naked stone, then forest, as far as the eye could see, until she turned west, where the village lay. The setting sun turned the snowy fields to fire, and Rosa could not take her eyes off the glorious scene. If she but had the skill to paint such a sight, she would be able to look upon it always.

But sunset meant more than just golden light. Sunset would give way to dusk, and she had a knight to find.

If the man still lived by the time she found him, for searching the forest at night was an impossible task for anyone, even a witch who could fly.

And if she didn't find him alive, at Midwinter…she would need to find another man.

Muttering a curse against all brave, foolish men, she headed out.

# Eighteen

A scream sliced through the air, startling Chase out of his doze. Whatever it was, it hadn't sounded human.

The sound came again, accompanied by the drum of hooves that sounded exactly like a horse breaking into a gallop. Or trying to.

His horse.

Chase twisted, trying to see his mare. Moonlight lit up the clearing almost as bright as day, but it did not penetrate the canopy behind him.

Short yips and barks came out of the bushes

— the sound of excited dogs. Then a third scream, that ended in a gurgle.

The sickening crunch of bone.

The wolf had killed his horse.

The last thing he'd had left of value. Fury rose up, at fate, the wolf, and everything in between. Chase would not let them take everything from him. Not while he still had a strong right arm.

He began to climb down the tree.

He slipped a few times, including the last few yards down the trunk, but he did not care. He would kill the wolf, and buy a new horse with the reward.

Chase reached for his sword, then thought better of it. The sound of the blade sliding out of the scabbard would alert the beast to his presence. Better to use a well-placed arrow, once he could see the creature.

He took a deep breath, put an arrow to the bowstring, then peeked around the trunk he'd tied his horse to.

A pair of glowing eyes regarded him.

Then another.

And another.

Dozens of eyes glowed in the dark, all pointed at him.

Excited dogs, his half-asleep brain had told him. Not dogs. Wolves. A whole pack of them. All staring at him over the carcass of his horse.

He bolted.

Chase clawed his way up a tree, then slid painfully down it, hearing a crunch as he landed. Then pain exploded in his leg, blinding him.

In the dark, he couldn't see the source. Had a wolf closed its jaws on his leg, bringing him down for the pack?

No. He wouldn't die here, a dog's dinner. He reached for the branches above him, hauling himself up by his arms alone, even as his muscles screamed in pain. But he could not stop – he'd seen dogs jump this high, and wolves were no different. He needed to climb higher, so they couldn't reach him. Up and up and up, until he emerged into moonlight again, at the top of the tree. He sighed and sat down heavily. Surely this would be enough.

The branch beneath him bent, then snapped, spilling him out into space. Out of the tree, and into the waiting jaws of the monsters below.

# Nineteen

Rosa headed for the clearing where she'd laid her trap, figuring it was as good a place to start as any. If the knight had heard from the Baron's men that they'd tracked the wolf that far, then he might have had the same idea as she had.

A scream told her she was heading in the right direction. The wolf had caught something tonight, though that hadn't sounded human.

It was not yet full dark, but the shadows beneath the tree canopy hid much. She flew lower to get a closer look.

Her blood froze in her veins at the sight of not one wolf, but at least a dozen, tearing at their prey, which appeared to be a large buck. No, a horse, she realised with deepening horror.

The knight's horse.

The man could not be far away.

As if reading her thought, a tree shuddered violently to her right. Almost as if some large creature had slammed into its trunk, trying to uproot it like the wolf had her perch yesterday.

Something cracked. A moment of silence, before the tree shuddered again. Now she could see something scrambling madly up the tree. A tree with whip-thin branches, that even she would not have climbed, for it would not hold her weight.

The knight fell.

Rosa didn't pause to think whether she'd be able to reach him in time. She had to try.

Offering up a prayer to the gods of the forest that she would survive this stunt, she swooped beneath the branches.

# Twenty

Chase was pretty sure death wasn't supposed to hurt this much. He'd remembered stories of paradise and angels, not pain. Unless he'd somehow found his way to hell. But that couldn't be right. What mortal sin had he committed to end up in eternal torment? Falling out of a tree didn't count. Perhaps accidentally shooting that queen had earned him such a punishment.

He was warm, too, which had to mean hell.

Chase sighed. Abraham would laugh himself sick. Though he was likely here somewhere, too, for killing kings was just as treasonous as shooting queens. Probably more so.

He forced his eyes open and stared up at…wooden boards, not stone. Well, the priests back home had never been able to describe hell. Maybe it was all wood, the better to burn sinners with.

But the only fire here burned merrily in a stone fireplace, which had a pot hanging on a hook above the flames.

Somehow, he'd expected more screaming in hell. Not the happy crackle of a cooking fire.

Then the door swung open and a red cloaked figure strode in.

The devil himself, surely.

Chase shrank back against the bed beneath him. "Mercy," he whispered. "I did not mean to hurt her. I swear it. Ask the princess. She knows."

Then the figure turned to hang up the cloak on a hook by the door. It wasn't the devil at all, but the white-haired witch.

"You!"

She set her hand on her hip, for the other carried a basket. "And who were you expecting, Sir Knight? Some princess, perhaps?"

He shook his head. "No, she saved me once, though I did not deserve it. She won't do it again." His mind finally caught up with his mouth. "Did you save me from the wolves?"

She set her basket down on the table. "Of course."

"Why?"

She stared at him for a moment, before saying slowly, "Because it was the honourable thing to do. Saving an innocent from the dark side of a forest he does not understand."

"I'm no innocent," Chase protested.

"No?" She scrutinised him. "So you'd prefer for me to take you back out there, into the forest? Maybe stake you out in the snow for the wolves to make mincemeat of you as they did your horse? If you don't freeze to death first, of course."

Only now did Chase realise he was naked beneath the blankets.

She'd removed his clothes? What kind of woman...

"My, what big eyes you have, Sir Knight,"

she teased. "Be easy. I have no intention of healing a man, only to send him to his death. You are safe here."

"What did you do with my clothes, wench?" he demanded.

She folded her arms across her chest. "It's Mistress Rosa to you, you ungrateful lout. And 'twas not I who shredded your clothes, but you yourself, running and climbing and falling through the forest. Why, when I found you, you were wearing little more than rags. You would have died if I hadn't found you."

Saved by a woman. Again. Chase felt his cheeks grow hot. "Thank you for saving me," he mumbled.

She waved away his thanks. "No need to blush like a maid seeing her first cock." Realisation dawned in her eyes. "Is that what has you so embarrassed? No need to worry so much, Sir Knight. As a healer, I've seen many such, and I know these things shrink in the cold. Perhaps now you're warm, I can better take your measure..." She reached for the blankets, a wicked look in her eyes.

Chase clutched them like his life depended

on it. "I'll thank you to keep your eyes off my cock!" he said hotly. Though now he thought about it, he wouldn't refuse if she put her hands on it...

Rosa chuckled and returned to the table. "Ah, I've already seen it. You're a fine size, nothing to blush about. But if you're the modest sort, maybe you should cover it with the blankets when I check the stitches in your leg. They should come out soon – your leg is mending nicely."

"You practised sewing on my leg?"

"Not so much practised as stitched the flesh together so it would heal." She reached for the blankets again. "Here, I can show you, if you like."

"No!"

She shrugged. "Suit yourself, then, Sir High and Mighty. I think I preferred you when you were unconscious. But now you're awake, I suppose you'll be wanting breakfast, so it's a good thing the hens laid plenty this morning."

While Rosa busied herself with making breakfast, Chase risked a peep under the blankets. Bandages covered his right leg, and encased most of his chest, as well. Broken ribs, he guessed, and his head hurt something fierce, too.

He watched the woman bustling about, and another, more pressing question came to him. "How did you manage to save me?" he asked urgently. She was half his size. She couldn't have carried him out of there, or fought off an entire pack of wolves.

Rosa grinned. "Magic."

"Magic doesn't exist," Chase said. Even he could hear the lie in his words.

Rosa set both hands on her hips. "It doesn't, does it, Sir Knows-a-lot? Then how do you explain this? I was flying past, when I heard a commotion in the woods, and when I came in close to see what was going on, I saw a man falling out of a tree, in a fall so great it would have killed you. So I magicked you up beside me, and flew you home here, so I could tend your wounds."

"People can't fly." This he was more sure about.

She looked smug. "I can."

That could not be true. "How did you carry

me here, then?" he challenged.

She jerked her head at the corner, where an old willow broom leaned against the wall. "Flew you back on my broomstick, of course. Don't you know that's how witches travel?"

Come to think of it, he had heard of such a thing. But it was such an impossible idea – brooms that flew – he'd never given it thought before. "Truly?" he asked weakly.

She shot him a look. "No, you daft thing. Sitting astride a broom is the stupidest thing I ever heard. Why, the wind would go right up my skirts and freeze the very core of me, it would. I'd need to bed a man every time I flew just to warm myself up again, and have no time for healing anyone."

He had to admit, her words conjured up such a vivid picture that he was more than a little aroused. In fact...

"Oooh, what a big – "

"Don't say it!" he begged, trying the cover the tent he'd pitched in his blankets.

To her credit, she didn't laugh this time. Instead, she shrugged. "Suit yourself, Sir Chase the Chaste. Anyone would think you'd never bedded a woman before." She considered him for a moment. "When you're healed, I could introduce you to a couple of girls at the inn who might be able to help you with that."

More images popped into his head, making him harder still.

He gritted his teeth. "Please, Mistress Rosa, can we talk about something...anything else? I was already in enough pain before this, and now..."

She blinked. "Oh, of course! You're about due another dose of medicinal. I almost forgot. I'll go down to the cellar and fill a jug. That should give you the time you need to...take care of things. Oh, and there's a bowl of water and a cloth beside the bed, so you can wash up after you're done, seeing as you're the modest sort who won't want my help with it." She winked as she knelt to lift up a trapdoor in the floor, then descended the steps until she was out of sight.

Chase shook his head. What sort of woman talked about sex as brazenly as this one? Most of the women back home had been more...modest. He didn't know what to think.

One thing was for sure, though - he'd never met a woman like her.

# Twenty-One

In the cellar, she sat down on a cask and laughed silently until tears streamed down her cheeks. So much for the brave and bold knights from her mother's stories – or even the show he'd put on for her that first morning. Perhaps she should not have kept him unconscious for two days, for she dearly needed a laugh.

Then again, if she'd let him wake earlier, he'd have been in a lot more pain. She'd used a fair bit of magic to heal him while he'd slept – magic the man did not believe in.

And strangest of all...he was the first man she'd ever met who wasn't eager to have a girl handle his man parts.

So much for spending Midwinter with the man. He'd probably shrink right up like a snail at the very thought.

Impulsively, she called out, "Are you finished, Sir Knight, or will you need a hand from me in finishing off?"

"I'm fine – fine! Just a moment!" he shouted back, in a fair panic.

She headed deeper into the cellar, to where her grandmother had kept the casks of medicinal mead, stronger than the usual stuff, and infused with healing herbs. Making more would take months, so she would have to be careful not to run out, but this would dull his pain better than the sleeping potions she'd given him before.

She wouldn't mind a cup of mulled mead herself, come to think of it. There were plenty of ordinary barrels she might tap. The knight would not mind a few minutes more to himself, either, she'd wager.

When she finally climbed the stairs, the

knight said, "You sure took your time. I said I was finished a while ago."

Rosa shrugged. "I didn't hear you." She set the jugs on the table.

"I shouted loud enough for them to hear me in the village. Gods, what did you do to me? This hurts! I'd give my kingdom for some wine to dull the pain."

She poured him a cup of the medicinal. "Try this. Then you'll owe me your kingdom, Your Majesty."

He didn't take the cup. "I have no kingdom. Not even a horse, now. What sort of knight does that make me?"

"One who's going to drink his medicine so I don't have to listen to you complain." Rosa thrust the cup at him, then folded her arms across her chest until he'd drained it. "There. That'll knit your bones a little more, if the magic's still as potent as I remember. Maybe your ribs will heal by the end of the day."

The knight choked. "That's not possible!"

"With magic, almost anything is possible. For a price." A blood price, usually, though she did not tell him that. This wouldn't be the first time she'd spilled blood for a stranger, nor would it be the last.

His eyes narrowed. "You sound wise for someone who looks so young. How old are you?"

Centuries, she wanted to tell him, but suddenly she didn't want to play with him any more. "I've seen twenty-two summers, but magic brings its own knowledge with it, wisdom from ages past. And witches learn young that power must be controlled, or there will be consequences."

"You're younger than me. Younger even than Maja was when..." The knight closed his mouth abruptly.

"Was Maja your princess?" Rosa asked.

The knight snorted. "Maja was my sister. She died in childbirth."

"I'm sorry," Rosa said automatically, then added, "Did the child die with her?"

"No, the boy lives. In a royal court, ward to the queen, no less. My brother in law could not have done better for his son." The knight shook his head.

To mention royalty so casually, this knight

must be highborn indeed. Ever so much higher than the Baron's family. And he hadn't said that his sister wasn't a princess – perhaps she'd married a prince, for her child to join the royal nursery. What must he think of her, and this cottage? Why, the man must be used to castles and golden plates. No wonder he hadn't wanted to take her clay cup.

She was lower than the servants who'd brought him breakfast in the morning. Speaking of which…

"I should do something with those eggs. Are you hungry, Sir Knight?"

"Chase," he said.

She mustn't have heard right.

"My name is Sir Chase. Call me Chase," he explained.

Rosa nodded. He surely understood proper protocol better than she ever could. "Breakfast, Sir Chase?"

"Yes! I feel like I haven't eaten for days. Why, I could eat a whole horse."

Did she dare mention his horse?

His face fell before she'd opened her mouth. He remembered, then.

"Just Chase. I'm hardly a knight at all without a horse. How the mighty have fallen." He shook his head. "Mistress Rosa, grateful though I am for your care and hospitality, I cannot repay you. The horse and what was in her saddlebags were all I owned in this world. Perhaps you should have left me to the wolves."

She recognised the despair in his tone. Her spirits had sunk that low at times, too.

"If you wish to offer payment, I'm sure you'll think of something suitable. I have helped far poorer patients than you, and they manage to find a way to show their gratitude. As for your horse...it seems to me the Baron owes you one, seeing as you lost yours in his service. Things are not so dark as they seem, Sir Chase. Your horse did not survive, but your saddlebags did. Your belongings are over by the window, and when you are well enough to leave your bed, you may have them back."

He half rose. "My cup? You have my cup?"

She rummaged through the bags until she found a metal cup. But when she drew it out, it glinted like it was made of gold.

Not just golden plates. Golden cups, too. This man was no ordinary knight.

"Thank you, Mistress Rosa. You don't know how much this means to me. It is all I have left of home, to remind me of them." His eyes turned pleading. "Can you stow it safely away again? I don't want it damaged."

She did as he bade her, wrapping it in the blanket that had covered it before.

She busied herself with breakfast, but bread and eggs were nowhere near enough to stop her mind from wondering what sort of man the gods had brought into her home.

Oh, he'd not harm her, she'd make sure of that, but whatever could bring a highborn knight, uncle to a prince, if he was to be believed, to hunt wolves in her woods, must be a curious tale indeed. A tale that he would tell her, she resolved, before the winter was over.

The least he could do after she saved his life.

# Twenty-Two

Chase had tried sitting up while the girl was in the cellar, but his ribs had hurt so much, he'd lay back down again, heartily wishing he'd never heard of wolves or witches. Not that young Mistress Rosa was anything like he'd expected. Young and pert and far too knowing for one so young.

Unless she'd lied about her age, but he doubted that. She liked discomfiting him with the truth far too much.

Nothing he said or did seemed to discomfit her...except when she'd seen the cup. Maja's cup, that Abraham had turned to gold at a touch.

If her eyes had taken on a greedy glitter at the sight of so much gold, he would not have been surprised, but she'd looked…saddened. Disappointed, perhaps? So, out of respect for his hostess, he'd asked her to hide it again.

Her good spirits had returned as she bustled about, stoking the fire and seeing to breakfast. She hummed a little as she worked, but it was no song Chase recognised.

If he closed his eyes, he might be back in the kitchens of the castle where he and Abraham had fostered together, hoping for a treat from the cook before being sent back up to the Great Hall to serve at table, as a good page should.

But those days were gone, and Mistress Rosa's humble cottage would not yield the same fare as a castle kitchen. Likely he wouldn't see meat again until he was well enough to return to the Baron's house.

He would find a way to repay her, he promised himself. Once he'd killed the wolf and received his reward from the Baron.

"Can you sit up?" she asked, setting a plate on the table.

She didn't wait for an answer, slipping an arm behind his back to lift him with unexpected strength.

Chase gritted his teeth against the pain he expected, but it never came. He stared at her in surprise.

"That medicinal mead's powerful stuff, is it not? I told you it would heal you by dinnertime." She winked. "Ah, but there's no such thing as magic, is there?" Her mischievous eyes dared him to admit he'd lied about believing in magic. She'd seen the cup. She knew.

"All the magic I've seen up 'til now has caused nothing but grief, so you'll forgive me if I am not so ready to believe it can be a force for good," he said, turning his gaze to his plate so that he might avoid those knowing blue eyes. Yet even the plate wasn't what he'd expected – for even the Baron's table had been set with trenchers of stale bread. And what lay upon it...fried eggs, slices of some sort of spiced sausage, several slices of fresh bread, though there was no butter. He automatically looked across the table, even as he told himself he'd be lucky to get butter here.

Her sharp eyes missed nothing. She grinned as she bit into a piece of bread, thickly spread with something white. She chewed and swallowed before she said, "I wasn't sure if you'd want cheese or butter with your bread, so I set out both." She pushed two bowls toward him. "I think I put too much honey in the ricotta, so it's sweeter than it should be, but I find a little extra sweetness in the morning is not such a bad thing."

He stared at his plate. His belly growled at him to eat all that lay upon it, but he could not. "I cannot accept all this, for I cannot pay you for it. Mistress Rosa, I cannot in conscience let you empty your cellar for me. Please, take some for yourself."

She burst out laughing. "Sir Chase, if you ate ten times that much, you could not empty my cellar, not if you stayed here a year. Now. You lost plenty of blood before I got you home, and you will need your strength. Mine will be ready soon, and then I'll join you." She headed over to the fire, tipping the contents of a pan onto her own plate. Not quite as much as she'd served him, but the sausage and eggs were plain enough to tell him he'd been mistaken about her.

He waited no longer, taking up his eating knife to devour the food before him like he hadn't eaten in a week.

Then again, he wasn't sure how long he'd been asleep.

"Healing yourself does work up an appetite, for magic can only do so much. The rest is up to you. There's more bread and I can fetch more sausage, but you'll have to wait until tomorrow for more eggs. Eat your fill, Sir Chase." She handled her eating knife with all the delicacy of a court lady.

She didn't belong in a hovel on the outskirts of some tiny backwoods village.

"Who are you?" he asked. "And what are you doing here?"

She set down her knife, her eyes widening with surprise. "Why, Sir Chase, you must have injured your head worse than I thought. I am Mistress Rosa, the witch of these woods, and when you fell from a tree, I rescued you and brought you here to my home to heal you. I thought to share a pleasant meal with you before I commence my work for the day, while you rest. But perhaps I should check your head first." She reached for him.

Chase caught her wrist before she could touch him. "Not before you answer me. What have you done to me? How did I get here?"

He became aware of something sharp pressed against his throat. He glanced down, and found himself staring at the hilt of his own knife, floating in the air.

"What are you?" he whispered.

Her eyes seemed to glow. "I'm a witch who doesn't take kindly to threats. I may have saved your life once, but that doesn't mean I'll hesitate to take it back. Especially from such a poor guest, threatening your host when I have spent the last two days healing you. You're lucky I have a greater grudge against the wolves than the momentary irritation of the insult you've offered me."

It was like facing Queen Margareta in the court of Aros all over again. Except this time he had nothing left to lose. Chase sagged. "Then I must beg your forgiveness, though I do not deserve it. Magic has meant ill luck for me at every turn, so that I cannot recognise anything else. I have nothing left to offer but myself, and I am poor compensation for anything. Yet...I pledge my sword and my honour in your service, until my debt to you is paid."

Custom required him to kneel and lay his blade at her feet, but he had no idea what had become of his blade, and if he tried to get out of bed, all he would do is fall at her feet. So he bowed his head and hoped it would be enough. At least if she refused, his death would be swift, for he could still feel the blade at his throat.

"Now I know you have drunk too much of the medicinal mead. A highborn knight, pledging himself to a witch? You must have mistaken me for your princess, or someone else. I have no need of swords or service or men at all."

But he could not feel the blade any more.

"Rest and regain your strength, Sir Chase.

Maybe you'll regain your wits along the way. You may stay for the week, but then I must send you on your way, back to the Baron." Her smile held sympathy – something else he did not deserve. Then she touched his forehead and sleep engulfed him.

Almost like some sort of spell.

# Twenty-Three

For a moment, Rosa almost regretted putting the knight into an enchanted sleep, but she banished the thought as quickly as it had come. She needed to take out his stitches and check how his bones were healing, instead of wasting time arguing with him.

Pledging himself in service to her, indeed! That had been the mead talking, more than the man. The only thing she could possibly use help with was killing the wolf, and what use was a man with a sword against an entire wolf pack?

But he hadn't been wearing a sword when she found him. Just the empty sheath. Oh, and he'd had a bow and quiver strapped to his back. Speaking about size, she'd never seen a bow so big. Taller than he was. She couldn't imagine how much strength it would take to draw such a thing, and he would need to heal some more before she could ask him to show her.

She changed the bandages around his ribs, noting with satisfaction that the bruising was already fading to yellow. With another dose of medicinal, they might have healed properly by the morrow.

She would have liked to leave the stitches in for another day, but she wasn't sure she'd get another chance if he woke up even grumpier than before, so she decided to take them out today, and mend the wound with a healing spell instead.

He might be a fool, blaming magic for his own ill luck, but she would not compromise her care on account of his foolishness.

When Rosa was satisfied that she'd done all she could for the snoring knight, she climbed up to the loft to check on the mead. As she'd surmised, the fermentation had finished and it was ready to be moved to the cellar to mature. That meant moving it from these casks to new ones, a task that would easily take the rest of the day, and perhaps the next, too.

By mid afternoon, she was lifting the barrels through magic alone, for her arms ached more than she cared to admit. Yet she'd dealt with more than half of the mead, so there would be less to move on the morrow.

Rosa floated the newly filled barrels to the cellar, then rolled them into place at the back of the cellar, where they would not be disturbed until they were ready.

If she had time on the morrow, she'd try her hand at turning the remaining barrels in the loft into extra strong, medicinal mead. She had to do something close to home, what with Sir Chase here in her cottage.

But such things could definitely wait until the morrow.

Sir Chase slept through the dinner hour and past dusk, so Rosa finished off the remains of the bread and sausage without cooking anything, and climbed into bed.

Her last thought before she fell asleep was that at least there was one benefit to having Sir Chase stay – it was warmer at night.

# Twenty-Four

Chase could not remember the last time he'd slept in a bed so warm. Maybe when he'd been a boy, and shared a bed with his brothers on the cold winter nights. The sound of their even breathing had lulled him back to sleep then, but the sound of someone else breathing beside him set his every nerve on alert now. What was the witch doing to him?

He reached out, and his hand closed over something soft and warm.

Her breast, he realised in horror, yanking his hand back, but it was too late.

"Yes, that's a breast, Sir Chase the Chaste. Your mother had them, and if you ever find the courage to propose to a woman, your wife will, too."

He'd touched fabric, not flesh, but the thin shift had left nothing to the imagination. "Why are you in my bed in nothing but your underthings?" he demanded, feeling his desire rising even as he tried to think of something, anything, else but the near-naked woman lying in bed beside him. Close enough to touch...

"Because it's my bed, you fool. Even with you taking over most of it, there's still space for me."

Shame washed over him. Of course it was her bed. A place he had no business being, even if she'd put him here.

"I'll sleep on the floor," he mumbled, sliding a leg out from under the blankets. Cold air chilled his flesh, but honour gave him no choice.

"You will not. You'll freeze your man parts off, and other bits, besides. I haven't tended you for days to let you freeze to death on my floor."

Impossibly, her arms wrapped around him, pulling his body against hers.

Soft, warm flesh, with only a thin shift between them, her breasts pressing against his back, tempting him, taunting him...

"But...your honour..." he began, trying to pull away.

For a woman, she was uncommonly strong. More magic?

"My honour? What about yours? Isn't that the mark of a knight, his high honour? Surely you can find it in yourself to be honourable enough to share a bed with a woman without molesting her in the night. At least, I thought you would be. Was I mistaken, Sir Chase the not-so-chaste?"

The taunt stung, especially as his thoughts were anything but honourable.

"You were not mistaken," he said stiffly. "If I but had my sword, I could lay it between us, for honour's sake. Forgive me for touching you...where I did. If I had but known you were there, I would not have reached out. It will not happen again."

She laughed softly. "If I have to choose

between sharing a bed with a sword or risk being woken by the occasional caress, I'll choose you and your wandering hands, Sir Chase."

He felt the blood rising in his cheeks, and other places besides. Thank all that was holy he had his back to her.

Her breathing soon returned to the even pattern of sleep, but Chase lay awake for a long time.

When he woke groggily the next morning, he found the bed empty. A sense of loss skimmed through his mind, too fleeting to catch.

Chase shook his head. She was right. He had suffered a blow to the head, and it had turned him into a fool for sure.

# Twenty-Five

For the third night, Rosa dreamed of Midwinter night, and the rite she was required to undertake if she wished to take her grandmother's place as priestess. Only a few days hence, and the gods had given her a man who would be living under her roof that very night. Almost as though they wished she would choose him.

A far better choice than Alard, for the knight would soon leave. The highborn knight probably thought peasant women shared their beds with noblemen like him as a matter of course, and he'd probably never think of her again afterward. A good thing, she told herself as she forced herself out of bed.

Rosa crept outside in the predawn light, holding her cloak tightly closed against the cold. She longed to return to bed, and see if she could wake the knight with a well-placed squeeze or caress. She'd done more than that in her dreams, and so had he. She laughed softly. No man could be as good as her dream lover had been with his hands, even if last night he'd worn the face of Sir Chase.

With Midwinter approaching, she shouldn't be so surprised the gods of the forest were sending her such dreams. Better that she spend the day working outside, for the more time she spent with the knight, the more likely she was to say something about his prowess in her dreams. Or how much she'd liked the feel of his hand on her breast last night. His touch had been surprisingly gentle, even as it set her heart alight.

She blamed her mother's tales of knights and princesses, chivalry and other such nonsense. Tales for normal girls, like Lule and

Piroska, for whom marrying some nobleman was the highest ambition they might have, but not suitable for a witch.

Her grandmother's tales had taught her far more, about the woods, and the history of this place, and magic. So much about magic.

But the tale uppermost in her mind now was about mead, and how one winter it had been so cold, the mead froze in the castle cellars. When the brewer had skimmed off the icicles and poured the remaining liquid into a new barrel, she'd found the mead more potent than anything she'd brewed before. The goddess of winter had blessed her brew, she decided, and offered up barrels of mead to her at Midwinter every year. When the longest night of the year ended, the Midwinter's Night mead was the best and strongest of all.

So Rosa had left some barrels outside last night, hoping they might freeze, and they told the truth of her grandmother's stories – frost rimed the sides of the barrels, and a thin layer of ice floated on top of the mead. She skimmed off the ice, poured the first barrel into a fresh one and dipped a cup into the liquid to taste it. Sure enough, it was stronger than the stuff she'd cellared yesterday.

By the time she was done with all the barrels, the sun was up, and the ice in the empty barrels had melted, so she left the casks in the sun to keep them from refreezing as she headed to the barn to milk the goats and fetch the day's eggs.

When she left the barn, he stood in the cottage doorway, squinting at the sun. Not naked any more – he'd found his clothes, and managed to put them on. He must be feeling better.

But that didn't mean he should be walking on that leg yet.

She opened her mouth to order him back to bed.

"Good morning, Mistress Rosa," he said, bowing, before he walked toward her.

He did not wince like a man in pain, nor did he limp. He was healed, Rosa decided, breathing a sigh of relief. Perhaps she could heal a man after all. Though that medicinal mead had definitely helped. She must make some more.

"Well met, Sir Chase. I was just fetching something for breakfast." She lifted the egg basket.

He frowned. "I should carry that for you. Leave it here. I will be but a moment…" He scanned the clearing, as if looking for something he'd lost.

Rosa smothered a smile. "The outhouse is that way." She pointed.

The knight flushed, muttering his thanks, as he loped off toward the outhouse.

# Twenty-Six

Rosa's eyes sparkled with unusual brilliance this morning, like the sun glittering off blue ice. Her cheeks were pink more from cold than any blushing at his fumbling in the dark last night. Perhaps she'd forgotten it.

He wished he could. Even washing in the icy well water hadn't helped.

She finished her breakfast quickly, then headed back outside. She returned with a paddle loaded with two loaves of bread. She dropped these on the table. "Careful, they're hot," she called over her shoulder on her way out. Two more loaves soon joined the first two, whereupon Rosa enveloped one in a cloth and began to cut thick slices from it.

"Now this is what butter was made for," she said, spreading it thickly onto the heel of the loaf. She bit into it before the butter could melt. "Mmm."

Chase gripped the table with both hands. Watching a woman eat had never done this to him before. Maybe if he jumped into the well and stayed there until everything was numb, he'd manage to cool his ardour.

"Help yourself," she said. "After watching you break your fast yesterday, I hope I've made enough."

She lingered long enough to grab a second piece before she departed again.

Chase deliberately took his time finishing breakfast, thinking about all things cold and as unlike the young witch as possible.

It didn't help. The moment he was done, she entered the cottage again, this time headed for the ladder to the loft.

"Sir Chase, would you go and stand by the fire for a moment? I'd hate for you to get in the way. If I broke your ribs after all that effort healing them, I'd be a poor host indeed."

He headed for the fire, happy to warm himself while she did...whatever it was. It sounded like it involved moving something heavy. It was on the tip of his tongue to offer to help, but a gust of wind rushed through the open door. He headed to close that first.

"Oh, by all that's holy...stand aside or be it on your head!"

Chase whirled at the sound of her voice and froze, transfixed. A row of barrels floated toward him, supported by nothing but air. Headed for the door behind him.

Now her words made sense. Chase leaped out of the way, just in time, as the barrels floated outside, then landed neatly on the ground.

Rosa slid down the ladder, looking annoyed. "Did you not hear me, or did you simply not listen?"

"How did you do that?" he stammered.

She swore. "Magic, of course!" She waved her hand and another gust of wind came through the door, swept up Chase's empty plate, then dumped it into the washing up tub by the window. "Just like that!" She reached for her cloak, which flew into her hand from across the room. She fastened it as though it was a perfectly ordinary occurrence. "I should have taken you back to the Baron instead of bringing you here. Let you heal normally instead of…" She raked a hand through her hair. This close to her, Chase could see that it was pale gold, not white at all. "Pack your things. Let me know when you're ready to leave and I'll take you back to town." She turned and marched outside.

Magic. Of course. The most normal thing in the world for a witch.

For all he'd seen – Abraham's curse, then mindreading royalty in the court of Aros…he'd never truly seen magic performed in front of him. Not like this.

That first day he'd woken up in her house, she'd told him she could fly. She'd probably floated him back here like one of those barrels. So many times he'd questioned her, and she had answered. If only he'd listened.

She had more magic than Abraham and the

court of Aros combined. Magic she'd used to help him.

And he owed her a debt for it. A debt he'd sworn to pay.

He followed her outside. "You can't take me back to town. I haven't repaid you yet."

She knelt beside a firepit, watching a wisp of smoke curl up from a pile of kindling. Then she rose, turning to meet his eyes as the flames behind her leaped into the air, fanned by the wind. Rosa didn't even blink. Instead, she folded her arms across her chest, challenging him to continue.

"I pledged my service, and you said I had a week. A week to repay you." Chase took a deep breath. "I will do anything you ask of me. Just as I would for my liege lord, or lady. Anything. Just name it. But don't take me back to the Baron yet."

It shouldn't matter whether he stayed here or at the Great House, but somehow…it did.

He'd said it before, but now he meant to do it properly. Chase fell to his knees and drew his dagger, which he laid across both hands as though it were his absent sword. "My life and my blade, I pledge it in your service, Mistress Rosa," he said.

She stared at him for a long moment, before she finally said, "By all the gods, Sir Chase...no one's ever done such a thing for me before. I'm no queen. I wouldn't rightly know what to say to that. Except...if I made a joke about the size of your sword, would you consider it a mortal insult? Because that's all I can think about right now."

"I have no idea," he confessed. "I've never made such a vow to anyone before, either." Not successfully, at least. Best if the King of Aros forgot he'd ever existed.

Rosa held out her hand to help him up. "I guess I accept, then. It feels ungrateful not to."

He wet his lips. "You should probably know that I am better with a bow than a sword. Oh, I can wield a sword well enough in the practice ring, but my accuracy is deadly with a bow."

He'd sparked her interest. "I saw your bow, and wondered...perhaps we can both use some target practice, but not today. Today, I want to try and get the god of fire to bless my mead."

That wasn't something you heard every day. "What can I do to help?"

# Twenty-Seven

Loath to admit this was the first time she'd ever distilled mead on her own, or that it had been years since she'd seen her grandmother do it, she asked Sir Chase to fetch enough firewood to keep the cauldron boiling for several hours.

While he did that, he would be too busy to notice she was not as sure of herself about this as she wished. Oh, setting out the cauldron and filling it from one of the barrels of fermented mead was easy enough, once the fire was hot enough, but setting the special lid on it just right was a more delicate task. Not to mention making sure she had a cask on hand ready to take the distillate, but far enough away that the cask didn't catch fire, and the liquid didn't evaporate.

Her grandmother had always lit the firepit closest to the herb garden, and placed the cask on the far side of the garden wall, Rosa remembered, so Rosa did the same.

Then she sat on the wall to watch the knight hauling barrow after barrow of wood. He favoured one leg over the other – as she expected, for while he'd healed enough to walk, he still had not healed completely – and more than once, he'd winced as the load he carried was more than his half-healed ribs could handle. She half expected him to complain at being forced to do the work of a lowly woodcutter, especially in his condition, but the man simply smiled as he passed her and kept going.

A smile that warmed her heart, each time she saw it. Watching him work, she thanked the gods for sending her such a man in time for Midwinter. Why, she might even enjoy her initiation now.

When he'd piled up enough wood to fill all four firepits, he perched on the wall beside her and asked, "Do you think we have enough to summon your fire god now, or will he want a bigger pyre before he puts in an appearance?"

Rosa laughed. "He doesn't actually appear," she admitted. "It's more of a story my grandmother always told, about the ways to make the best mead. The recipe originally came from the goddess of bees, but the god of fire and the goddess of winter had a competition one Midwinter, to see who could make the best mead..." She stopped at the knight's sceptical look. "You're of the new faith, aren't you? The one with only one god, who cures diseases, conjures bread and fish, walks upon the surface of water without falling in and can raise people from the dead? The god of the desert people in the south?"

Chase nodded. "That sounds like the tales our priest told, yes. A faith more than a thousand years old is hardly new."

"It is new here. And the more people who believe in it, the fewer will respect the old gods, or give them their due. Then they grow angry, and it falls to we few who remain to remember the old ways, to save those raised in the new faith from a wrath they cannot begin to understand." Rosa shook her head. "Those who spread the new faith say the old gods are evil, but truly, they are not. Only when they are angered or not shown proper gratitude for their gifts do they stop caring for their people…but surely that is not evil. If you cared for someone every day, and never heard a word of thanks from them, only insults when they did not ignore you altogether…would you not turn away from them, too?"

It would be so easy to ignore the needs of the village, to live her life as she wanted, without taking up the mantle of priestess to the gods of the forest. Especially when even the village children taunted her…

"I'm a knight, not a god," Chase said slowly, "but if people hated me, I admit I would not want to help them, either. Yet…many of our priest's tales told of forgiveness, and charity, and how we should help those who needed it, not just our friends. Perhaps because if the other gods withdraw their assistance, it is up to us to perform their duties." He wiped a hand across his eyes. "Alas, I am no theology scholar. I learned to wield a sword and shoot a bow. Who am I to know a god's thoughts, or the reason they do what they do?"

His words put her to shame. Who was she to question her fate, indeed? She had received her magic as a gift from the gods, and she owed them her service for such a blessing.

"But I have heard many stories from my father's bible. What I have not heard is a tale about a mead-making competition between gods. So, Mistress Rosa, must I beg for this tale, or is it only told at Midwinter?"

A blush stole across her cheeks. "No, Midwinter is when...when they drank the mead. The tale is told whenever it's time to make it." She eyed the cauldron, which had not yet begun to steam. "I suppose we have plenty of time."

She took a deep breath. "The goddess of winter and the god of fire were drinking mead together one cold winter's night. The offering was made to the goddess, in thanks for helping a brewer, and the goddess said she would show the god of fire how to improve on the nectar of the gods, for that's what they called mead.

"She spread her magic around the jar, until ice formed on the outside. When she lifted the lid, the contents had frozen over, like a lake in winter. But just like a lake, when she smashed a hole in the top, there was still liquid inside, sweeter and more potent than before. She lifted out a jug of the stuff and shared a cup with the god of fire, who proclaimed it as his new favourite drink.

"He drained his cup, then said fire was far better than ice when it came to drink that warmed you from the inside, and he would make something even better.

"The goddess said he was welcome to try.

"So he took another jar, and built a fire beneath it. Soon, the jar began to boil. He took his sword and shield, placing the shield atop the bubbling jar, and propping it up with his sword, held upright in an empty jug." Rosa gestured at her setup. A conical copper lid with a pipe at the top, which slanted down to the empty barrel on the other side of the wall, was a far cry from the sword and shield, but if she closed her eyes, she could almost imagine it being the first such still, before time and practice had refined it to what she had now.

"My grandmother said the sword and shield were made of bronze, which glittered like gold," Rosa added.

Something tightened in Chase's expression, as if he did not like this particular detail.

Rosa hurried on. "The steam touched the shield and turned to liquid. The droplets ran down the sword until they formed a rivulet, filling the jug with what looked more like water than mead. Yet when they drank it…it burned their throats like liquid fire.

"The goddess said that ordinary mead had the power to heal, so this stuff was so medicinal, it could cure anything, so she declared that the god of fire had won the contest.

"He poured himself a cup of the sweet mead from the goddess's jar, and said the mead he'd made by fire was so strong, so pure, it should not be drunk by mortal man except on the very cusp of death. A mead most men could not drink was hardly mead at all, and he declared the goddess had won the contest.

"They then proceeded to drink more mead, as they argued about who had won the contest. By the time they had drunk all the mead, they had forgotten all about the competition, and it was time to…to do what deities do at the Midwinter solstice…so they never declared a winner." She ducked her head to hide her blush.

Chase laughed, his good humour returned. "I love it! Gods who get so drunk they forgot to pick a winner."

Rosa smiled, happy to let him believe it. If she told him why they'd been too distracted by their other duties, he would be horrified. Sir Chase the Chaste would not understand the power of fertility rituals, especially between gods.

He waved at the cauldron. "So you are making the fire mead today. Why not the ice mead?"

Rosa pointed at the barrels lined up outside the cottage. "I left those outside last night. I skimmed the ice off them while you were still sleeping, when I lit a fire in the baking oven for our bread. We call it Midwinter Night mead, for the goddess, and usually it stays in the casks for another year before it is drunk the following winter. The flavour is richer."

"And what will you do with the fire mead?"

This part was the bit she understood the least, for no matter how well her grandmother had explained it, Rosa had not been able to grasp how it was possible.

"The distillate – which my grandmother called the raw spirit, for it feels like your very soul has been ripped out of your throat when you drink it – is mixed with magic imbued leaves, so steeped in healing magic it is said they could bring a man back from the brink of death." She thought of the Baron – why had Grandmother not given him the medicinal mead? Unless she knew it would not work, for his growth disease could not be cured by it. There was so much her grandmother had not had time to tell her. "Perhaps that is what your desert god used. Maybe they knew the secrets of distilling there, too. Or your desert god stole the secret from our fire god."

"I'm not sure what intrigues me more. Gods getting drunk and stealing from one another, or magical, life-saving leaves. I wish I'd had some when my sister was dying. I might have been able to save her." Chase's shoulders slumped.

"You can't save everyone. Sometimes, it is simply their time." Rosa closed her eyes. "But sometimes, it's not. It's every bad decision you and everyone else ever made, that rips someone from you before their time. And no matter how much you wish you'd done things differently, that maybe you'd been brave enough to go instead of them, or you'd been quicker to take action in the past when it might have made a difference…it is still too late. I would give anything to have her back, and yet I still know I couldn't save her."

"Your grandmother?" Chase guessed.

Rosa nodded, not daring to raise her eyes lest he see the tears spilling down her cheeks. It did not do for a witch to show weakness.

"Was it sudden?"

Another nod. "The first snows had just fallen. We didn't even know the wolf had come down from the mountains. He killed her on the road, on her way home."

He stared at her. "You mean…the wolves the Baron sent me to kill? Your grandmother was killed by a wolf pack?"

"It was only one wolf then. The same wolf who killed my family, the last time the snows came. The same wolf I tried to kill the day before you came, but I thought it was just an ordinary wolf. I should have listened better to her stories…" Rosa shook her head, angry with herself. "It must have found a pack in the mountains and taken it over. Like…a man building an army…" Even as she said the words, they felt right. Like a man, not a wolf.

"A wolf building an army? Impossible. It was just a pack of them. Hungry, seeking food, and I foolishly left my horse where they could find it. I should never have left my eyrie. If I'd stayed up high, I could have picked them off one by one and I would have already claimed the Baron's reward." He jumped to his feet. "I shouldn't be sitting here, sharing stories by the fire. I should be out there, with my bow, fulfilling my quest."

"No!" Rosa grabbed his arm. "You're not healed yet. You've barely been out of bed for a few hours – you're in no state to go out hunting on your own. The medicinal mead may have brought you away from the brink of death, but it still takes days to heal. That beast out there is no ordinary wolf. There is magic about him, I tell you, or I would have killed him myself before you came. I tried, and failed, and barely escaped with my life. I could not kill one lone wolf, and you cannot defeat him with a pack at his back. If you were to go out there now, I might not be in time to save you again." She gestured at the still, which had started to drip. "Besides, don't you want to taste for yourself, and see which of the old gods truly makes the best mead?"

Five days. She only had to keep him here for five days. Long enough for Midwinter to have come and gone, and for her to have kept her word to Alard. But she would have to keep her word to the Baron, too, and become a priestess at Midwinter. For that, she needed the knight.

"Please, Sir Chase. You have travelled to

many places, and undoubtedly tasted many fine things. Perhaps you can settle the score between the goddess of winter and the god of fire. Perhaps they will see fit to offer you a blessing that may help you in the coming battle."

"The bishop back home would have me excommunicated for even thinking about accepting your offer."

Hope sparked in her breast. "But you are considering it, are you not?"

He stared at her, as if measuring her soul. "More because it is foolish to refuse a drink offered by a beautiful woman, than because some deities I do not believe in may offer me some kind of magical assistance."

The knight had turned the tables on her, for he was far more skilled at flattery than she would ever be. "You go too far, Sir Chase. No man has ever called me beautiful and told the truth in the same breath."

"Then it seems the men of your village are more foolish than me." He took a deep breath. "It is said far and wide that Queen Margareta of Aros is the fairest lady any man has ever seen, but I have gazed upon her face and I can honestly say you bring more joy to my eye in a moment than a lifetime spent in her presence."

Rosa didn't know what to say. She managed a shy smile. Finally, she said, "Then I thank you for the compliment, Sir Knight."

Perhaps her mother had not been wrong about knights and their courtly courtesy after all.

# Twenty-Eight

He didn't deserve her thanks. He hadn't lied, but…he hadn't told her the truth about the Queen of Aros, either. Then again, no one here needed to know the truth about how he'd been banished from Aros. Least of all Rosa, whose ice-fair features were lovely enough to tempt any man. Including the Baron's son, he was sure.

A thought that shouldn't send a rush of anger through him, yet there it was. He'd experienced jealousy before, envying Abraham and Maja their happiness together, but that was nothing compared to the acid eating his insides now.

Even as he told himself he was here to complete a quest and earn a reputation, a tiny voice in the back of his mind added how wonderful it would be to win Rosa's heart along the way. To share her bed the way a man usually did with a woman, dishonour be damned.

Only he would have to leave her at the end of the winter, for he had no place here. And to break the heart of a witch who could probably kill him with a glance, or curse him for the rest of his days, did not seem like the wisest course of action.

The Baron's son was a better match for her, he reasoned. She could rule over the Great House instead of this tiny cottage, and have servants to do the work for her. And surely she had family here, for in a village so small, everyone must be related to some degree.

Unless the wolves had killed them all.

But why would a wolf do that – kill a whole family, yet leave the rest of the village untouched? Until now. It made no sense.

"What can you tell me about the wolves?" Chase asked, trying to sound casual.

"Well, there was only one until the day you decided to go after him," Rosa said.

One wolf? That's what the Baron's son had said. But for one wolf to kill so many people...

"How many men had it killed before the Baron sent for me?" he asked.

She stared at him, as though trying to decide if such a question merited a reply. Finally, she said. "He killed my parents and my sister, six years ago, and my grandmother a few weeks ago. There are tales of others he may have murdered in the past, but that was long ago. Too long for anyone to know for sure. Then there's you, and me, though he hasn't killed us yet."

"The wolf attacked you, and you got away? How?" The moment the question left his lips, he knew he'd been stupid. "Wait, I know — magic, right?"

He'd earned a smile from her as she nodded.

"Can you tell me more than that? If there is some way I can defeat it, then I must know more." He reached out and captured her hand.

"Please, Mistress Rosa. You've told me tales about gods getting drunk. Now tell me the tale about the beautiful young woman escaping from the beast."

"That is another story entirely, and not the one you want, I think. But if you wish to know the true tale of the reckless witch who went out to kill the wolf by herself, you shall have it." Rosa took a deep breath.

He listened to her tale, which sounded disturbingly like his own plan when he'd headed out to that clearing. He'd seen the feathers, but dismissed the earlier kill as something the Baron's hunting party had placed, not Rosa. The more she spoke, the more his admiration grew. If the wolf hadn't manage to knock her out of her tree, she would have been victorious, he was certain of it.

"No wonder the wolf sought reinforcements before it fought you again," Chase said in wonderment.

Rosa blinked. "But that's just it. Wolves don't do that. They are either part of a pack, or they aren't. The only lone wolves who are allowed to join a pack are either fertile females or a male so strong he defeats their leader, and any other challenger the pack sends against him. Only a man – a leader of men – would go and recruit an army to defeat a foe they cannot defeat alone. In wolves, they would see that as weakness and slink away to find a more easily conquered food source. They would not return with greater forces. Wolves don't think like men…unless magic turned a man into a wolf, as my grandmother said."

"Is that possible?" He didn't want to believe it, but after all he'd seen Rosa do with her magic, he might have to.

"My grandmother told many tales of such things, long before my gifts revealed themselves, so that I might recognise my magic when it came. Neither of us expected my powers would have an affinity for air, and it took me longer to master than others might have because it seemed like such a trivial thing at first. Then I learned I could use it to listen, and lift things and…on the night I fled from the wolf, I truly learned to fly." Rosa spread her hands wide. "So, I suppose my answer is that yes, it is possible. Transforming people into beasts is a common method of punishment, when a man commits a crime against a witch."

She said it in such a matter-of-fact way that it shouldn't have sounded like a threat, or even a warning, but Chase shivered all the same.

In a soft patch of dirt beside the fire, the cat rolled onto its back, stretching as it dozed in the warmth.

"What was his crime?" Chase asked, pointing at the cat. He could easily imagine the beast as some fat, greedy baron, taking everything from his people and leaving them to starve.

Rosa stared at the creature. "Oh, Hagen's crime is laziness. When a rat entered the cottage, he let it get away with Grandmother's dinner."

"She kept a man in her cottage to catch rats?" Now he'd heard everything.

Rosa laughed. "Of course not. Hagen is a cat, one who's supposed to be much more suitable for such things. But when he got all the female cats around pregnant so they were all busy with their litters at the same time, and Hagen would not hunt...she took his manhood." She grinned evilly. "One stroke of the knife, and no more kittens for him. I swear it made him even more fat and lazy than before, but Grandmother liked him sitting on her lap of an evening, so she tolerated him. I have yet to find a use for him. Perhaps he can warm my bed when you are gone." Now she wouldn't meet his eyes.

"Gone. Yes," Chase said vaguely. He'd barely been here a week, but already he didn't want to leave. He'd never thought such a tiny cottage could be comfortable, or even a desirable place to live, but with Rosa...he could not...nay, he did not want to imagine living anywhere else. Yet how could he already think of it as home?

He was becoming as mad as Abraham.

Better that she share her bed with a sexless cat than a less than honourable knight who half feared and half hoped he'd give in to his desires and make love to her in the night.

She'd probably turn him into a neutered cat for it, though.

Better that he turn his thoughts to besting the beast, and not her bed.

If Rosa allowed him to. She could easily have left him in her house, and gone after the beast by herself.

Chase cleared his throat. "When you hunt this wolf again, will you allow me to help you? I may not have magic, but I have yet to meet a better bowman than I. If I take care not to climb or fall out of my tree, of course."

"Modest, aren't you, Sir Knight? All right, you may show me your bow skills on the morrow. If you can match me, then I will agree to hunt with you."

From any other woman, the suggestion that he might not be good enough would have rankled. Yet the challenge he saw in Rosa's eyes made him want to rise to meet her.

Here he had no golden armour, no herald to announce him, not even a horse to ride. In his regular leather armour, with injuries that had barely healed, his fate rested on the best archery performance of his life.

Against a woman who could manipulate the very air so that she might fly.

"The size of your cellar! You have enough space and supplies here to feed a whole castle through a siege, and yet there is nothing more than a tiny cottage atop it?"

Ah. "This was once the seat of an ancient king, who built a mighty fort in the forest, the home of his gods. When conquering invaders came from the south, he made an alliance with them. Their builders and architects took apart his wooden halls and walls, finding the weaknesses they could exploit in other, similar forts that held their enemies, and rebuilt his in the style of their own brick and stone palaces, so they might winter in comfort and safety in between campaigns.

"Eventually, the southerners headed home, carrying the wealth of the king's neighbours, but leaving the king his share, and the palace. The southerners never returned – my grandmother said they lost their own city to invaders, while they were out waging war here – so the king ruled alone. One of his descendants moved the capital to somewhere more convenient for trade with the northern cities, and the forest was allowed to conquer the castle."

Chase nodded. "Then why is the cellar still here?"

She hadn't thought to ask that question when she'd first heard the tale, but then Grandmother had captured her imagination with tales of battle, kings and princes. Then, she hadn't known how slowly a house fell into ruin, or how the upper parts collapsed into the cellar until…

Rosa wiped away a tear, chiding herself at thinking of her parents' house, when she should be thinking about this one.

"The kings left much of their wealth hidden here in the cellars, ordering the stones of the palace to be pulled down and carted to where the town is now, so that none might stumble across the king's treasury by accident. A cottage was built atop the entrance, home to the High Priestess dedicated to protecting the grove…and the king's people from the wrath of the forest gods."

She managed a wry smile. "Grandmother once told me the High Priestess was chosen from among the king's daughters, for the gods demanded no less than royal blood be shed at their altars for granting the king their favour. She laughed and said that meant we had royal blood, too, for she never would have been chosen as High Priestess without it. If it is true, then perhaps I am a princess, too." She stuck her nose in the air, trying to look as haughty as Piroska. "But as I have yet to hear of a princess who milks goats, I won't start wearing a crown any time soon." Or ever, she added silently to herself. Though she had played with some rather corroded ones in the back of the cellar when she was a little girl.

No need to tell the knight that the old king's treasury still hid in the secret chambers beneath his feet. Forgotten by all but herself, now.

Chase climbed the steps and stood before her. "That is a pity. A circlet of fine silver, studded with rubies, would keep your scarlet hood in place in the winter, but for summer, a fillet of gold set with sapphires the icy colour of your eyes, I think, holding back your hair so that all might see your lovely face and lose themselves in your eyes as I have. I should write a letter to the king, come spring, commanding he honour your beauty as it deserves."

She met his gaze squarely. "You're mocking me, Sir Knight. What would your princess think, if she knew you said such things to me?" She turned and headed back to the fire, for while he'd been stoking her ire, the flames were in need of feeding.

Behind her, she heard him mutter softly, "She is not my princess, and may never be." A sigh with the weight of the world upon it accompanied his words.

Her heart went out to him – for he loved a woman he could not have – but she didn't stop to offer her sympathy. If he'd meant her to hear, he would have spoken louder.

Let him think he kept secrets. Like the pain in his eyes as he hefted the next cask. The man would not be able to draw a bow on the morrow, and another day in bed might help him heal completely.

She'd give him a cup of the freshly fire-distilled mead when all was done, to help ease him into sleep tonight. She might even drink a cup herself.

# Thirty

Dawn burned Chase's eyelids, while some bloody minstrel had started drumming on the inside of his head. His bladder begged to be emptied, but he had no desire to release the warm, soft maiden in his arms.

Even her hair was soft, and she smelled of honey. No surprise, given all the mead they'd brewed yesterday. And the mead they'd drunk…

By all that was holy, he hadn't dishonoured her, had he?

He should have felt a stirring in his groin at

that thought, but with her body pressed against him, as it likely had been for hours, he was already hard as a rock.

Oh, now he definitely needed to visit the outhouse.

When he returned, Rosa had already lit the fire, and she had a pan in her hand, ready to warm it to make breakfast. She pointed the pan at him. "What manner of mischief were you up to out there? Doing more damage to yourself, after yesterday?"

He flushed, torn between telling her why he'd taken so long in the outhouse, or lying and saying he felt fine.

"Bed for you, you bad boy, and if you try to get up again, I'll tie you to it," she said.

He wanted to argue, but he hurt too much to stay stubborn when he really wanted to go back to bed. If he went hunting today, the wolf would win for sure.

He climbed into the bed and pulled the blankets up to cover himself. He might have taken his time in the outhouse, but watching her walk around the cottage in a thin shift, her nipples clearly visible, would soon arouse his desire again. He forced himself to look away.

"What was in the mead we drank last night? Miners, with picks and hammers, I swear, for my head is full of them this morning," he said.

"I told you 'tis no good to dull the pain so, or to keep working in your condition, but you're a stubborn one, Sir Knight. I'll make you some willow bark tea, if you swear you'll stay in bed." She set her hands on her hips, daring him to refuse.

Why did she have to stand so, thrusting her breasts forward so he could not help but stare at those two pink pearls?

Chase squeezed his eyes shut, but still the image taunted him from behind his eyelids. "As you wish, Mistress Rosa."

A cool hand touched his forehead, forcing his eyes open. "You feel a mite hot, Sir Chase. I hope 'tis not a fever. I'll fetch you some of the medicinal mead, too." Her icy eyes fair melted with concern for him.

Chase blamed the fever in his blood. He cupped her cheeks, stretched up and kissed her.

Her lips were warm and soft, as he knew

they would be, tasting slightly of salt.

She'd broken her fast already, without him.

Disappointment welled up, and he dropped an arm around her to pull her closer. Her breasts touched his chest and he lost all reason, kissing her as though beyond her lips, she kept the very air he needed to breathe.

And she returned his kiss, yielding to his embrace as her tongue curled to tempt his, for this maiden was as skilled with her mouth as she was with her hands. Oh, to feel either of them on him, to...

She broke the kiss. "Sir Chase. I thought I'd made myself clear – I want no swords in my bed." She climbed out of his lap and resumed making breakfast with her back to him.

Swords? He glanced down at the all-too-obvious tent in his tunic, outlined by a damp patch where she'd been sitting. Either she'd shared his desire, or he'd made a mess of things. Again.

Strongly suspecting it was the latter, Chase hung his head. "I'm sorry, Mistress Rosa. You are so enchanting, I forgot myself. For a moment. It won't happen again."

She hung a pot from a hook over the fire, then glanced over her shoulder at him. "That's a pity. For you have quite an extraordinary mouth on you, Sir Chase. Not to mention a clever tongue. I imagine your princess is very fond of your kisses."

He wanted to shout that he had no princess, but the noise would have hurt his head, and she wouldn't have listened, anyway. Yesterday, she'd said she had royal blood, which meant if he wanted to kiss any princess, it was her.

Now, if Rosa had agreed to become his princess…

Chase lay back and imagined how she might grow very fond of his kisses indeed…

# Thirty-One

Two days she kept the knight in her bed, and two nights she slept in his arms. More than once, she'd considered climbing into his lap, lifting his tunic and finishing what they'd started.

But she knew she could not. If she succeeded in seducing him, he would stare at her after, his eyes wide with guilt, and swear he would not let his desire overwhelm his reason again. And that simply would not do, with Midwinter approaching. If she could spend but one night as his lover, best to save that pleasure for Midwinter. For she'd be lying to herself if she thought she might want to spend the night with any other man.

So after two days of letting the magic-infused mead do its work, she didn't protest when she came in with the morning's milk to find him stringing his bow.

"I won't repay my debt to you lying in bed," Sir Chase said, his eyes on the notched yew. "I mean to help you slay that wolf, so that I may keep my word and complete my quest."

She almost told him that if he gave himself to her tonight, the longest night of the year, he would help her more than enough, but something in the stiffness of his back and shoulders made her bite her tongue. Honour and pride – a man's worst failings, though most men considered them virtues – would force him out after her if she left to slay the wolf alone. Gods only knew how that would end, especially if the pack found him first.

"I'll go clear the snow off my archery targets, then," she said lightly, heading back out the way she'd come.

He stared at her, his mouth open as if he

wanted to ask something, but the only words that came out were an abrupt, "Thank you."

Rosa scoured the ground of snow, but the archery targets were nowhere to be seen. Come to think of it, she couldn't remember the last time she'd used them. Certainly not since she'd learned she could simply fire an arrow in the vague direction she wanted, and command the wind to do the rest. Perhaps her grandmother had added the targets to the lumber pile, and they'd become buried under some woodcutter's payment for services rendered.

She finally found them atop the woodshed roof, covering holes the thatcher had not yet seen to. She set the targets up in front of the bramble hedge that would be a mass of berries when summer came, and found Sir Chase watching her from the cottage doorway.

"Most men set targets up in an empty field, or at least somewhere with plenty of clear ground to make it easier to retrieve the arrows that miss the target," he said. "I can't imagine you want to venture into the brambles, nor heal my scratches if I do."

"I never miss," she said.

He gave her a long look. "Neither do I."

Chase strode up to the furthest target, then paced the distance across the clearing. He turned, took aim, and fired.

His arrow hit high, halfway between the centre and the edge.

Before Rosa could comment on his accuracy, he fired off a second shot...one that buried itself in the very centre of the target.

By the time he'd emptied his quiver, Chase had marked his target with a cross made of arrows. Then he bowed, like she imagined a knight would to his lady-love at a tourney. "Your turn, Mistress Rosa."

She shook her head. For a moment, she'd thought...something very silly indeed. "Of course."

She took her time stringing and testing her bow, ducking her head until her blush faded. He might be a knight, but she was no lady. She was the kind of girl he might allow to warm his bed for a night, before forgetting all about her.

Rosa let her first arrow fly, biting her lip for the air she needed to carry it where she wanted. She fired off a half-dozen more, until she'd roughly marked the rune for the winter goddess on her target. The goddess was far more powerful than some deity who made fish multiply. Why, the fish themselves could do that.

"Not bad," Chase said.

Rosa folded her arms. She'd been every bit as good as him.

"Let's try again," he said. With four more arrows, he turned his cross into the rune for the fire god.

Rosa's mouth went dry. Did he know...?

"Now, your turn," Chase said, setting the butt of his bow on the ground.

Rosa lifted hers, ready to bite her lip again.

"Without magic," Chase added.

She stared at him in horror. "Why in the goddess's name would I do that? You use your strengths, and I'll use mine."

"But what if you need to use your magic for something else, and can't use it to guide your arrows? Better that you use your bow to shoot, and shoot well, and keep your magic for where it's most needed. What if you grew tired, or you ran out of magic?"

Rosa shook her head. "Magic doesn't work that way." But even as she said it, she could see he had a point. She could grow too tired to use her magic properly, or she might lose too much blood and be unable to cast another spell. And while she could summon a huge gust of wind, she struggled to control two, even if they were very small.

"Show me how you shoot, Mistress Rosa. Please."

Between the look in his eyes and his wheedling tone, she could not refuse him anything. Thank the gods he hadn't asked her for a kiss instead.

Rosa took a deep breath, released it, and focussed on her arrow. It would never reach the target from this distance without magic.

She fired anyway, seeing the arrow dip so that it would strike the dirt long before the target.

He hadn't said anything about not using magic to retrieve her arrow, though, so she dashed forward, ready to catch the arrow when it flew back into her hand.

When she'd halved the distance, she took aim once more. The second arrow reached the target, but only just. The point touched the bottom edge, then fell away, for it had not hit hard enough to stay.

Rosa cursed and summoned the arrow back.

"I'm too far from the target," she said, lifting her foot to halve the distance again.

But a hand caught her arm, pulling her back.

"I assure you, you're not," Chase said, releasing her. He held out his arms. "May I show you?"

Mutely, Rosa nodded.

She found herself pulled into his embrace, or that's what it felt like, until she realised he had his hands on the bow and arrow, not her.

A hard, muscled leg slid between hers, making her gasp, but he merely nudged her stance wider as he turned her, then withdrew.

Rosa couldn't breathe. She'd lain in his arms for several nights now, but somehow this seemed closer, more intimate. Then she felt his body hard against her back and she thought she might swoon.

He laid his cheek against hers. "Pull," he

whispered, wrapping his hand around hers as he drew the arrow so far back, his fingers touched her breast. "Aim." He blew out a warm breath that seemed to head straight down the lacings of her gown. "Loose." He let go.

Rosa's knees crumpled. Fortunately, the only thing he'd released was the arrow – if anything, his grip around her tightened, so she stayed on her feet. Barely.

"Now you try," he said. "Or do you want me to show you one more time?"

Her voice came out as a whisper. "Please."

"First, I want you to promise me something."

"Anything." She meant it, too.

"You won't go off hunting the wolf without me. When you go, you'll take me with you. I want your word, Rosa. I can't bear the thought of you going out there alone. If something were to happen to you...so I must go with you. Give me your oath on whatever you hold holy that we will hunt the wolf together."

She pressed her lips together. While her body might be going mad with desire for this man, her head still ruled her. And she knew she would be safer hunting without him. Especially after tonight.

"Give me your word, or I shall carry you inside and lock you in the cellar. Then I'll hunt the beast on my own."

"NO!" burst from her lips. "You'll be killed!"

He chuckled. "A normal woman would be fearful of being locked up, while having faith that her champion would return victorious."

She wrenched free so she could face him. Why, oh why was she breathing so hard?

"If I were a normal woman, you'd already be dead. I won't let that wolf kill anyone else!"

His stony expression gave her no hope. "Your oath, Mistress Rosa."

She closed her eyes. This was madness, yet what else could she do? "I swear on my life, and the souls of my family, that when I hunt the wolf who killed them, I shall take you with me."

With her eyes still closed, she had no warning. He seized her and kissed her, stealing her breath almost entirely. For a moment, she froze.

It's Midwinter Eve, she reminded herself. If they spent the rest of the scant daylight hours kissing, when night fell he might be the one to seduce her, and with the gods' help for the hunt, he would be safe.

She gasped, sucking in air like a woman nearly drowned, threw her arms around the knight's neck and kissed him with all the passion she could muster.

# Thirty-Two

Hoofbeats, in a hurry. Chase reluctantly released Rosa, and took up a defensive position before her. He might only have a bow, but he could kill the horse and its rider before either reached Rosa. He had some honour left, after all.

The rider galloped into view, then pulled the horse to a stop, hard. "Sir Chase!" the man shouted, sliding to the ground. "We all thought you must be dead!"

Alard, the Baron's son. Chase lowered his bow. "Only thanks to Mistress Rosa here, and the good fortune that wolves prefer horseflesh to mine."

"Well, thank God for that, then, eh? Though you must be quick if you mean to kill the beast. I have sent out my men to scour the forest for it. After it attacked again…"

Rosa ducked out from behind Chase. "Who did you send? And who was attacked?"

"Mighty hunters, just like Sir Chase here, though I don't think any of them were knights. They rode off in different directions. Each man swore he would bring me the wolf's head, and win the reward." Alard looked dazed. "The beast will not survive the night!"

"You fool!" she hissed. "It's your men who won't survive the night! There's more than one wolf now – a whole pack of them, and they hunt horses!"

Alard's face turned pale, his eyes suddenly as icy as Rosa's when she was annoyed. "It's treason to show such disrespect to your liege lord, not to mention the man who will soon be your husband. Beg for my forgiveness now, and I shall not have you thrown in the stocks."

Rosa was betrothed to the Baron's son?

Why hadn't she told him?

Rosa gasped. "The Baron? He's...gone? How did the wolf manage to enter his bedchamber?"

"Of course the wolf didn't kill him. Wolves can't open doors. He died last night, on the blade of his own sword, which caused chaos in the household, for there was no priest about to administer last rites, and I feared for his soul..."

Rosa stamped her foot. "Let the priest worry about your father's soul. Who did the wolf attack, if not the Baron?"

Alard's face still looked pinched. "Piroska. We did not find her until this morning, what with all the fuss over my father. It's likely one of my riders scared the wolf off, or it might have been much worse."

"Worse than losing the woman carrying your unborn son and heir?" Rosa demanded, advancing. "Your father would be ashamed to hear you say such a thing. And you gave me your word that you would marry her before the week was out. Faithless fool, what kind of man can't even protect his own wife and child?"

Alard retreated, until his back smacked against a tree, his eyes round with fear. "She lives! She lives!"

Rosa stopped. "The wolves didn't kill her?"

"The beast dragged her into a ditch beside the road, her cloak so covered in mud no one saw her until morning, when she was half frozen. She has some bite marks on her arms, but that is all." Alard seemed to recover a speck of his former composure. "She is safe in her father's cottage, resting. He had to give her some strong drink to send her to sleep, for she was quite hysterical."

Rosa blinked, suddenly thoughtful. "Piroska does not own a cloak. She wraps herself in a shawl as she stares at me in mine."

"I gave it to her. She insisted she would not see me again until I gave her one," Alard said. "Just like yours."

Realisation dawned. That meant…

"The wolf mistook her for me," Rosa said slowly, as if reading Chase's thoughts. "If it doesn't know the difference, it will come back for her, to kill her as he did the rest of my family."

Chase found himself nodding. "Or perhaps it noticed it had made a mistake, and left her."

"It's an animal!" Alard said. "Beasts don't think!"

"Go home, Alard. Get Piroska into the Great House, then lock the doors and bar the gates. Post guards inside. We'll deal with the wolf, and maybe save the lives of your men while we're at it." Rosa flicked her hand in dismissal.

"As your husband to be, I forbid it!" Alard insisted. A stronger man might have roared the words, but Alard's voice was too reedy for it to sound like more than a whine.

Rosa lifted her chin. "You are not, and never will be, my husband. Now, get home, you fool, to the woman you promised you'd marry. Before the wolf pack comes after you and your horse."

Wind began to move through the treetops, swirling what leaves remained. Alard's horse's ears flew back, his eyes rolling in panic. The horse recognised angry magic, even if its master did not.

"I command you to come with me!" Alard said.

Chase watched in amazement as a whirlwind of leaves shot down to the ground, lifted a struggling Alard, and dropped him into his saddle. The horse bolted, its master barely clinging to its back, while the wind whipped the beast's tail to urge it on.

"His father was a good man who believed in the old gods, but paid lip service to the new god for the love of his wife. He should have taken another wife after she died, but he said he had no need, with Alard as his heir. Gods grant Alard a son who possesses all the wits he does not, though given who the mother is…who knows?" Rosa shrugged. "What he does now matters not. We need to find that wolf before it kills again."

Chase agreed. "Tonight."

She sighed. "I had hoped to wait until tomorrow, but we cannot. It seems I will definitely need your help, enacting the best plan we can concoct before sunset." She looked troubled, but didn't say why.

Probably worried about facing the wolf

again, after failing the first time. Chase certainly was.

"May your gods help us," he said solemnly. The god of his father certainly hadn't done anything for him – perhaps the old gods would be more helpful.

"They'll have to, if they ever want another priestess." Rosa beckoned. "We have a few hours until dark, and you promised me an archery lesson."

Chase wished he could lock her in the cellar, safe from harm, but Rosa probably knew another way out. She was as eager for this fight as he was.

He swallowed. No more kisses. He would bring her the wolf's head, or die trying.

# Thirty-Three

"That tree," Chase said, pointing.

He'd picked the largest one, with branches so broad you could sleep on them. The wolf would not be able to knock over this mighty tree, Rosa was certain of it. She brought the carpet lower, so that Chase only had to step out onto the branch. He had his bow, a full quiver, a jar of tallow and a brazier full of coals. His armour would protect him and his cloak would keep him warm. She shouldn't worry so, she told herself, but she could not shake the memory in her mind's eye of him falling out of the tree that first time.

Remember, we both have to survive this battle, if you want us to perform the Midwinter rites tonight, Rosa said silently to the gods of the forest, knowing they would be listening. Unless you wish to find a new priestess.

She didn't expect a response, but it would have been nice, all the same. The gods only spoke to the High Priestess, or so her grandmother had said.

She didn't have chickens as bait this time. Hagen had caught his first rat, and inadvertently showed her the nest where she'd found four more. Now their gutted corpses lay scattered around the clearing, the smell of fresh blood enough to lure any predator in for a taste.

She prayed it would be enough, and wished she'd had the foresight to demand Alard's horse to use as bait instead.

If they failed tonight, she would head straight for the stables.

She had her bow and a quiver of her own, but Chase was the true hunter tonight, not her. Her job was to be his eyes in the air, seeing what he could not, while his fire arrows would light up the clearing, bright as day.

The fire should drive off the pack, if they were naught but ordinary wolves, they'd decided, but they weren't so sure about the white wolf. Fire had saved her life the night it had killed her family, so it would surely be wary of it, but not in the way of a wild beast. No, like a man who had been burned.

Rosa flew up, high above the treetops, where she might see the clearing and half the forest. She pulled her cloak close around her, and settled down to wait.

The sun sank. The sky faded into twilight, before deepening to darkness. The moon would not rise for hours yet. All the more reason for the fire arrows.

The wind brought her sounds from every corner of the forest, whispering that wolves were on their way, and from where.

Rosa let the wind carry her own whispered words to Chase: "They come, from the west."

She thought she glimpsed something moving in the trees, around the edge of the clearing. The southern side, though, not the west. Then she blinked, and it was gone. Probably just leaves, or snow whipped up by the wind, she decided.

Chase's first arrow blazed into light, arcing up, across the clearing, to find its target in the eye of a wolf. He was a remarkable shot, and she would tell him so, when this was over.

His second and third arrows landed in the snow.

Perhaps not so remarkable, after all.

Two more wolves went down to ordinary arrows.

Only then did Rosa realise that the shots into the snow had not missed, but the lamp oil had been slow to catch fire. A ring of flames rose up, encircling the wolf pack.

The pack panicked, milling around the clearing like frightened sheep. One picked up a dead rat, while others ran in every direction, cutting one another off as they darted around, trying to escape the flames that fenced them in.

Rosa looked in vain for the white wolf, but it was nowhere to be seen. Once again, the creature had sacrificed someone else with no care for the consequences or loss of life. A nobleman or a king for sure.

She glanced at Chase, wondering if the knight would simply slaughter the pack while they were trapped. He was a nobleman, too, after all.

But the branch where he'd sat only moments before was empty.

"Chase!" she shouted, swooping lower.

"I see it!" he called back.

She could not see him, but his voice sounded excited. She dropped further, straining her eyes to see. Was that movement on the ground beneath it? Gods, if he was on the ground…

A fire arrow dropped into the snow, narrowly missing the white wolf's tail. It started to run away.

"I have a clear shot!" Chase said, now on the tree's lowest branches. Barely two yards above the snow, level with a drift that stood between him and the beast. Almost like a defensive wall…

The wolf came barrelling back the way it had come, charging up the drift. If it leaped, it would land on the same branch as Chase, or push him off it to his death amid the crazed pack.

The wolf bunched its muscles, and Rosa dived to intercept it.

Paws scrabbled for purchase as it landed on the end of her carpet, claws digging in to the weave. With shaking hands, she nocked an arrow to her bow. At this distance, she couldn't miss.

The wolf snarled and snapped at her, sending her scuttling back to the trailing edge of the carpet. It lunged, now half on the carpet. If it got its hind legs up, it would kill her for sure.

She fired, nocking arrow after arrow as she urged the carpet to buck the beast off.

She reached for another arrow, just in time to see her quiver roll over the side, out of reach.

Rosa gripped the sides of the carpet, closing her eyes as she turned the air into a whirlwind. She clung on for dear life as it dipped and spun, desperate to shake the wolf off before it reached her. But the beast's claws were snagged in the carpet – it just wouldn't fall.

Then something smacked into her head, and she knew nothing.

# Thirty-Four

Chase watched in horror as the carpet spun crazily between the trees, Rosa and the white wolf clinging to it. If he could only get a clear shot…for he could not risk hitting Rosa.

There. If the carpet spun one more time…he fired, and had the satisfaction of seeing his arrow sink into the beast's paw, prying it loose from the carpet. The creature fell, hopefully to its death.

He turned his eyes back to Rosa. She'd slumped facedown on her carpet, which was now falling out of the sky. He raced to catch her, but she fell into a deep drift of snow before he could reach her. Chase didn't stop until he'd dragged her out of the snowdrift and into his arms.

She was as limp as a corpse, but she still drew breath. She lived.

But there was blood in her hair from where she'd hit her head. He needed to get her home, where she had that miraculous medicine that had healed him. Hopefully it would heal her, too.

He glanced around, hoping to see the wolf's body, so he'd know where to come and collect the head in the morning. But his arrows had burned out, and he couldn't see much. He found a snapped-off pine branch, sticky with pitch, and plunged that into his brazier to use as a makeshift torch.

Carrying Rosa and the torch was a struggle, but he had to make it home, and there was no other way. Her magic carpet would not fly until she woke, and he had no horse.

So he set one foot in front of the other and

trudged into the forest, hoping and praying he would find his way.

# Thirty-Five

Rosa woke in unfamiliar warmth, though it took her fuzzy head some time to realise why it felt wrong.

"Sir Chase?" she whispered.

A gentle hand touched her forehead. "Does it hurt?" he asked.

"No," she said. "Should it?"

"You flew into a tree and knocked yourself out on a branch, I think, so I brought you back here. I gave you some of the same mead you made me drink to help me heal."

Medicinal mead? No wonder her head felt

fuzzy. But it didn't hurt, either, which meant he must have given her a lot.

"What about the wolves?" she asked urgently.

"You shot the big one full of arrows and he collapsed in the snow, dead. The rest of the pack ran off when the lamp oil burned out." Chase paused. "I figured we could go back for the body tomorrow, or whenever, but it was more important to get you home to bed, as I didn't know how badly you were hurt."

She remembered now. She'd been so busy trying to shake the wolf free that she hadn't noticed where she was flying.

"How long was I out?"

If she'd slept through Midwinter Night, the gods of the forest would definitely be displeased.

"Maybe an hour? I came straight here, and gave you the mead, before I even put a fresh log on the fire. It's still burning, look." Chase pointed.

Relief washed over her. It wasn't too late.

"Then we should celebrate," she said, pressing her lips to his.

She half expected him to pull away, but he returned her kiss eagerly, cupping her head in his hand to prolong it.

Rosa let her hand trail down his chest to the hem of his tunic. He wasn't ready for her yet, but a few pumps of her hand and he would be.

"Hey!" Chase pried her hand off his cock. "You've had a lot of mead, Mistress Rosa. I'm not sure you're thinking clearly."

"But it's Midwinter Night," she said impatiently, reaching for him.

Chase jumped out of bed, backing toward the fire with his hands up in a shield against her. "Now, that's no reason to get drunk and give in to all our desires," he said cautiously.

Ha! So Sir Chase the Chaste had been entertaining lustful thoughts for her. Good.

"Of course it does – it's Midwinter Night!" When he still looked mystified, Rosa continued, "Remember when I told you the story about the mead competition between the god of fire and the goddess of winter?"

He nodded.

"They drank so much mead they forgot to name a winner?"

Another nod.

"That's the children's tale my grandmother told me when I was younger. You see, the goddess of winter was a maiden, and all the other gods wanted her for a wife, because she was also a fertility goddess, but she wanted none of them. She was a huntress who hunted alone. They'd all tried to woo her, but failed. The fire god, being a trickster at heart, waited until all the others had given up, and he joined her for a drink when she came back after a long hunting trip. That's when he issued his challenge."

Chase still looked puzzled.

Rosa went on. "They had their contest, each proclaiming the other the winner. And every time they did it, they toasted their win with another cup of mead. Cup after cup, until they'd drunk most of the jars dry. Then the god of fire began to woo her in earnest. Complimenting her on her beauty, her skill at the hunt, anything he could. Then he laid a wager that he could kiss better than she could.

"Of course, the drunk goddess kissed him. She liked it so much that she did it again, and again. Each time they kissed, he gave her a breath of his heat, until she was so hot inside, she took off all her clothes. But they kept kissing, so she started taking off his clothes, because his skin was as hot as hers. He let her do it, until they were both naked.

"Then she insisted upon taking him for a roll in the snow to cool him off. So she took him to the snow in the far north, and beneath him, the snow began to melt until it had formed a pool around him. Then the water began to steam and bubble, turning into a hot spring. So hot the goddess of winter feared for him, so she jumped into the pool to save him.

"She laid his body on the snow, terrified that his body had cooled too much, and tried to use her own body to warm his. Being the trickster he was, he was only pretending to be injured, so he immediately began to respond to her caresses with his own, until their shared passion overcame them both and…they melted the snow around them, which started the spring melt.

"Mortified at what she had done, the goddess went and hid her face, until winter came again the following year. She brought snow down to cover the land, hiding the scene where she'd shared such passion. But at Midwinter, the fire god returned, to share some mead with the goddess, and she wept so many tears of shame, she set off the spring melt again. But her salty tears turned the land barren, where nothing would grow.

"The following year, the fire god arrived early, and hid, where he could see her without being seen. The goddess thought he had not come, and drank the mead alone, bemoaning that the fire god was not there to share it with her, for if she was fated to melt her own snow just thinking about him, it would be better to share passion and make the soil fertile again.

"When the fire god heard this, he jumped out of his hiding place, finished off the contents of her cup, lay her down on the snow, and together they made love with such passion that all the snow melted early, washing away all the salt and making the land fertile again."

Chase was nodding once more. "I wish you could tell this to my brother. Back where I grew up, the sea flooded the land so often that whole swathes of it are lost to salt. He'd happily bow down and kiss your goddess's feet if she would make the soil sweet again."

Her shoulders slumped. He'd missed the point of the story. She would have to explain even more.

"In the villages, most people know the shorter tale, not the full story. The priestesses learn the full story as a novice, when they first spill their maiden's blood at Midsummer." She paused just long enough to see that this wouldn't be enough, then rushed on with, "But they do not graduate from novice to priestess until they have played the part of the winter goddess at Midwinter. First they must make the Midwinter Night mead, which takes a year, and when it is ready, they choose a lover.

"Grandmother said some of them chose a man from among the fire god's priests, or they were paired with a novice priest, but as the new faith took hold and there were fewer and fewer of us, more and more, the priestess picked her own lover. Unless she becomes the High Priestess, a lover is all she is allowed, for that one night of the year, so – "

"What about the High Priestess? Is she allowed to sleep with whoever she pleases?"

Rosa's cheeks glowed red. "No, of course not. On the years when there is no novice, she must take the place of the goddess. She may choose a lover, but as High Priestess, she is allowed to marry, as long as her marriage ceremony is performed in the old way, and only at Midwinter. The High Priestess and her husband reenact the goddess's first night of passion with her fire god lover, while the other priestesses..."

"Dance around naked?" Chase suggested.

Rosa frowned. "If you already knew, why did you make me tell the whole tale?"

Chase laughed. "I meant it to be a joke — I had no idea it would be true. Dancing naked in winter sounds like a good way to lose some toes, or worse. But there are stories, like witches and their broomsticks, that witches like to dance naked in the moonlight. I didn't think it would be wise to ask if it was true."

Rosa let out a breath she hadn't been holding. "All right, then."

Chase folded his arms across his chest.

"You still haven't explained what this has to do with you trying to seduce me."

Rosa pressed her lips together. "My grandmother was the High Priestess, and I am still a novice. There are no other priestesses, so I must take the role of the goddess tonight."

Silence swelled between them.

Finally, Chase said, "You want me to pretend to be some pagan fire god, and seduce you outside in the snow?"

Rosa could feel the emphatic NO about to leave his lips.

She forced a smile. "Actually, it doesn't snow much here, and as there isn't anyone else to dance or observe the rites except the gods themselves, maybe they wouldn't mind if this time, the rites take place in a bed." She swallowed. "Please, Sir Chase."

# Thirty-Six

Between the beseeching look in her eyes and her nipples poking through the thin fabric of her shift, Chase didn't know where to look. He'd be a fool to say no, but what sort of honour would he have left if he said yes?

"If you don't do this, it will be a whole year before the gods have a proper priestess. In their anger, who knows what they might do to me, or the village?" She took a deep breath, and his gaze darted down to her swelling breasts again. "Worse than a wolf pack. Perhaps they will send a dragon to destroy us.

It is said the fire god alone can control the fire breathing beasts."

So he'd be honour bound to defeat a fire breathing dragon after all. Good for his reputation, if he survived. If.

Chase opened his mouth to tell her he'd do it.

"You promised to serve me. A week, you said. If you do this for me, give me just one night, I will consider your debt repaid."

By all that was holy, yes! If she brought honour into it, he had no choice.

He tried to keep his expression calm, though he was singing inside. "When you put it that way, Mistress Rosa, then it becomes a matter of honour that I do as you ask."

Her eyes lit up. "Truly? You will help me?" She whipped off her shift and lay naked on the bed. "Then take me, Sir Chase. For tonight, I am yours."

Chase swallowed. Now was not the time to admit he'd never made love to a woman before. But for the first time in his life, he wished he had, for he wanted to do this right.

If her gods helped him to make this a night

for her to remember, he would serve them faithfully until the day he died.

# Thirty-Seven

Gods, Chase looked as nervous as she felt.

"So, we should maybe start with a drink, like in the story?" Chase suggested, pouring two cups brimful.

Rosa sniffed hers. "Which mead is this?"

Chase shrugged. "You're the expert, not me."

She took a cautious sip. "This is the medicinal mead. There's precious little left, and no knowing if I'll be able to make it as well as my grandmother. Best pour it back in the jug and put it somewhere safe. I'll go down to the cellar and find us something more suitable to drink." Clumsily, she wrapped a blanket around herself and headed down the stairs.

"Right. I'll...stoke the fire, so it's warmer up here, for when you come back," he called after her.

Definitely as nervous as she was. She considered backing out of the deal altogether, but she knew she couldn't. She had to complete the rites, so she could serve the gods as priestess. Nothing else mattered now.

She found last year's Midwinter Night mead sitting untouched, where she'd left it a year ago. The goddess runes on the barrels were wonky on some of them, as it had been the first year she'd made it. If she'd known a year ago that she would be using the brew in her own rite of passage...Rosa shook her head.

In her haste, she'd forgotten to bring a jug with her, so she decided to float the whole barrel up the stairs to the cottage. Probably for the best, as they might need more than one jug of mead to calm both of their nerves before the night was over.

She set the cask on the table, then knelt

down to tap the barrel. Her blanket kept slipping down, forcing her to yank it back up again, until she bunched it up in her fist to keep it in place. Try as she might, she could not tap a barrel with only one hand.

"Let me do it," Chase said, placing a second blanket around her shoulders. "You get back into bed, and warm. Unless half freezing to death is part of the ritual?"

Rosa shook her head. "I've never seen the ritual performed before. I know only the story, and how there must be mead, and sex."

Chase looked alarmed. "I'll…I'll get the mead, then, and you get into bed, ready for…the other stuff."

She felt the uncontrollable urge to laugh, but one look at Chase's face told her that might not be the best idea.

This was a mistake. Curse the gods for placing her in this position.

"If you don't want to, we don't have to," she said in a rush. "We can – "

He slammed the jug of mead on the table. "I want to."

"Oh." It was the tiniest sound, barely a

word at all, escaping without permission as she tried to assemble her scrambled thoughts.

He wanted...her?

Chase poured these cups more carefully than the first, not spilling a drop.

But when he handed a cup to her, Rosa's hands shook so badly she spilled it down her chest. She swore.

"Here, let me." Somehow, he'd found a cloth and a bowl of water, and he squeezed the water out of the cloth as if he'd been a healer all his life.

Rosa released the blanket, baring herself to the waist.

With the cloth, he traced the line of stickiness between her breasts and down her belly, then back up again, as if he couldn't decide which breast to wash first. His hand went right, but then he leaned over, peering at her left breast. The cloth rasped over one nipple as he took the other in his mouth, sucking hard.

She tangled her fingers in his hair. "Gods, Chase!"

He looked up, and his eyes were full of

mischief as they met hers. He let go, tracing a circle around her nipple with his tongue. "I'm not sure what tastes sweeter, you or the mead."

And then he kissed her mouth again, his arms around her, as he climbed into the bed beside her. She helped him undress, still kissing him, except when they had to stop to pull some item of clothing over his head.

Once he was naked, she could run her hands over his chest, stroking the firm muscles like she wanted to. Down his chest, his belly, and the hard length of him…

"Don't," Chase groaned, pulling away again.

"But…I thought…you wanted…"

He tipped her onto her back. "I want, all right, but if you get your hands on me like that, I won't last more than a moment, and I think for us to have sex, I must at least make it inside you."

She thought for a moment. "If you're so sensitive, then perhaps we should leave off on the stroking and sucking and move onto the sex."

"Are you sure? Are you ready for me?"

Before she could answer or even nod her

head, he'd slipped a finger inside her.

"Not yet." He knelt between her thighs, pushing them open wider, before he traced her lower lips with his finger, as if he was trying to memorise them. Then he touched a place that left her gasping, and she opened her eyes to see him grin. "That's the spot." He rubbed harder, and she thought she swooned, unable to focus on anything but his finger and what it was doing to her.

Her breath came in great, ragged gasps, as his finger sent ripples of desire rolling through her body. Bigger, and bigger...until she arched her back, digging her fingers into the mattress as she exploded at his touch.

She was still panting by the time her vision cleared enough to see his face. Still grinning.

"Rosa, I want you more than any other woman I've ever known. But I need to know if you're ready for me. If you want me."

He had his cock in one hand, ready to enter her, while his finger still stroked her lightly, sending small ripples through her.

Rosa swallowed. "If you're going to do that to me again, I'm not sure I'll ever be ready for it." When he frowned, she hurried to add, "But if you're asking if I want you to do that again, and to make love to me…then yes. As many times as you like."

He slid a finger inside her again. "You're wet enough, that's for sure. Tell me if I hurt you, Rosa, and I'll stop."

She nodded. The first time with Alard had hurt, but that had been mercifully quick, and from what Chase had said, this would be, too. Then he could back to doing the thing he did with his fingers.

Except…his fingers hadn't stopped, still rubbing her until her vision started to cloud again. Then she felt him enter her, in one slow, smooth stroke, stretching her but not hurting her.

But the ripples were getting bigger again, as she panted faster, clenching her muscles hard like she had before, only with Chase inside her that set off more ripples. Caught between the two, she was lost in love for him.

He started sliding in and out of her, no longer slow, and she lifted her hips to meet him, keeping pace as he sped up, until each frenzied thrust pushed her closer and closer to what felt like it would be an even bigger explosion and she couldn't stop but she wasn't sure if she could bear it when it did come and...

"Oh gods, Chase, Chase!"

Some time later, she opened her eyes to find him grinning at her again. She could still feel him inside her, but he'd stopped moving and somehow, she didn't feel quite so full any more. And she was shaking. Couldn't stop shaking. Didn't know why. And yet...

"That was amazing. I want to do it again," she said, her voice hoarse from...had she truly screamed his name?

He reached for the bowl and cloth. "First, let's get cleaned up. Then, I want to spend some time stroking and sucking, as you called it, before we find out if I'm even capable of making you scream like that again."

She winced as he eased out of her, hating how empty she felt without him. "My first time was nowhere near as good as that," she said, to distract herself from the way he stroked the cloth down his own length, before using it on her. "Are you a very experienced lover, or is that what royalty require from their husbands?"

He dropped the cloth in the bowl, then stared at her. "Well, I guess that explains why there wasn't any blood, and why I didn't hurt you, if I wasn't your first. But I wouldn't know anything about what royalty require from their husbands or their lovers. That was the first time I've ever made love to a woman, and it was better than I dreamed it would be." He filled the cups, and held out hers. "If you spill it this time, I promise you, I'll use my tongue to clean every drop that lands on your skin."

Rosa drank deeply, her hands no longer shaking. Oh, there was a little shiver of pleasure at his words, but not enough to shake the warm glow that suffused her whole body. She drank until only a few drops remained at the bottom of her cup, which she dribbled across the top of her breasts, meeting his gaze squarely with a challenge of her own.

Chase laughed. "If you hadn't done it, I was going to pour my cup over you. By all that's holy, I could spend all night just worshipping those breasts." He drained his cup and set it on the table. Then he pushed her down on the bed, touching his tongue to her nipple once more. "So sweet." A finger slid inside her, stroking, as his other hand closed on her breast. "And I want you wet for later, too, when we see if I can earn a better adjective than amazing."

"Yes. Oh, yes." Rosa wanted to say something more articulate, but with his hands, his lips and his tongue on her, she soon struggled to say anything coherent at all.

# Thirty-Eight

The sound of Hagen growling woke Rosa. Hagen never growled, unless there was another cat outside. Probably sniffing at the door, wanting to come in out of the cold. She didn't blame it. Even with Chase spooned up close behind her, she could feel the chill air. Almost as though the fire had gone out, or she'd left a window open. But the shutters had been closed for weeks, and she wouldn't have left...

The door was opening. Swinging out wider, until she could see the moonlit clearing outside.

Hagen had puffed up, until he looked more like a thundercloud than a cat, complete with ominous rumbling. Yet even he backed away from the door, retreating into the shadows beside the fire.

Rosa crept out of bed, reaching for the nearest weapon – the poker. She held it before her like a sword and demanded, "Who's there?"

Something huge and pale leaped at her, knocking her down. The poker flew from her hand, clanging down somewhere out of reach.

She saw firelight glint off big eyes and…even bigger teeth…

The beast had knocked the breath out of her, and with its weight crushing her, she couldn't even draw in the air to scream.

Air…

Cold air came screaming through the open door, pelting the beast with leaves as it tried to lift the creature off her.

But the beast seemed to be pushing down just as hard, its weight more than she could bear as those teeth came closer, and closer…

And then the weight was gone, as the beast

rolled off her.

Rosa jumped to her feet, backing away as she felt around behind her for anything else she could use for a weapon. Even the poker, which was surely…

But the beast didn't move. It just lay on its back, on top of the poker. No, not on top of.

"I wouldn't have thought a poker would go straight through him like that, like a greased spit," Chase said. He nudged the beast with his foot.

A paw curled, like a fist clenching in agony.

"Pull it out," Rosa said. "It will die a faster, more merciful death that way."

Chase shrugged. "If you wish." He reached for the handle.

"Don't," the creature said hoarsely.

Except…the white fur on its belly seemed to be thinning, exposing more skin. And the paw had lengthened, almost like fingers…

"Gods, it's a man!" she said, staring.

Only the head hadn't changed, and then she realised the massive man wore a white wolfskin cloak, with the stuffed head adorning the hood so that it looked like his face. Yet he shoved it aside and she found herself facing a wrinkled, white-haired man.

"You're not Mistress Kun," the old man said. "I thought I smelled her magic, but you're not her."

"I am Mistress Rosa, and I have some healing skill," Rosa began. "If you let my friend remove the poker, I might be able to save you."

"For what? A lifetime as a wolf, seeking the bitch who turned me into a beast? Better to let me die, girl. She killed the rest of my sons, as if that might bring back the one she whelped who died in his sleep." The man coughed. "She found me offering up the body to the gods' care, ready to light the pyre. Screamed that I'd killed him, and she'd kill all my sons and tear down all I'd built. After she'd made me watch all of it, she cursed me. Said if I could find her in the doorway to death, maybe I could be a man again. Ever since, I've been searching. Neither a wolf nor a man, and all I know is the stink of magic. But whenever I followed it…the witch would rather die instead of turning me back. And only now, I realise I must have heard her wrong. It wasn't her I had to kill to turn back into a man. It was me."

He squinted at her. "You look like my daughter, Skathi. She's the High Priestess to the winter goddess – even Kun wouldn't risk the wrath of the goddess by hurting her. Find her. Tell her to make sure to give me a king's funeral. Burned before the altar."

Rosa bowed her head. "It will be done."

"And give my cloak to your man there. He looks mighty cold."

Rosa glanced at Chase. He was as naked as she was, and he did indeed look cold. Perhaps if he closed the door...

The wolf had opened the door to the cottage. She'd always wondered how he'd gotten into her family's house, for the door had been closed when she found them. She opened her mouth to ask.

The wolf king gave a little sigh and said no more. Rosa checked his pulse.

"He's dead."

She didn't know whether to be relieved or sad. For years, she'd yearned for this, and now...

So this was vengeance. She'd thought it would be sweet, but it was as bitter and bleak as the heart of winter.

"What do we do now?" Chase asked.

Rosa swallowed. "We burn the body, like I promised. I guess I'm the priestess now, so it falls to me."

"To us," Chase corrected. "We're in this together. Until the very end."

# Thirty-Nine

Rosa seemed dazed, so Chase left her to pull on some clothes while he, already dressed, headed outside to find a handcart to carry the body to this altar she'd spoken of.

He should have felt as confused as Rosa, killing a wolf who'd turned into a man only to die again after telling the strangest tale he'd ever heard.

And yet…his mind was clearer than it had ever been. Seeing that beast slavering over Rosa, he'd known exactly what to do.

Even now, he could see his way forward,

knowing exactly what he wanted to do next.

He filled up the handcart with enough wood to make a pagan funeral pyre, then went inside for some other supplies. Rosa had pulled on a shift, but she seemed to be struggling with the laces.

Chase headed over to help. After making love to her tonight, he wanted to unlace her more than cover her up, but that could wait. She'd need to be dressed warmly, and if he had to dress her, he would. He found a clean overdress and helped her into it. Stockings, boots, cloak…

He left her sitting on the bed as he stripped the corpse of its cloak and carried it to the cart. The man, despite his age, had been powerfully built. No wonder he'd made such a huge wolf. As for his parting gift of the wolf head cloak…Chase could decide whether to accept it or not later, when the body was dealt with. Or leave it up to Rosa.

"Ready to go find this altar, High Priestess Rosa?" he asked.

She blinked and finally seemed to focus. "Just a priestess. Not so high," she said. She sighed. "I had everything so clearly planned out, and now…I'm lost. What do you do when you finally finish your quest?"

"Find a new one," he replied. "Or rest and recuperate for a bit, then think up something else to do."

She nodded. "Yes. I should…rest. Would you rest the winter with me?" Before Chase could answer, she continued, "Oh, but you probably have a new quest. Never mind. I would have liked…but it doesn't matter." Her shoulders slumped.

He would bring a smile back to her face. By dawn, if not before, Chase swore.

Ha. Yes, he did have a new quest.

Gods grant he would be successful in this one, too.

# Forty

Together, they threw the corpse onto the pyre they'd built on the ground at the foot of the stone altar. They piled more wood on top of it until it resembled a bonfire more than a funeral pyre. Then they stepped forward together and thrust their torches into it, setting it alight.

Rosa bit her lip, bringing a breeze into the grove to fan the flames. The quicker the corpse became ashes, the better, for the night was cold and dark, and it would be many hours before the sun would warm the land again.

She moved closer to Chase, craving his warmth more than that of the fire.

"Shall we go back to bed?" he asked, wrapping an arm around her.

She longed to say yes, but she could not. "We must keep vigil until all traces of the body are gone. You go home if you wish, and back to bed. I will join you once the fire burns to ashes." But not before dawn, for it took a long time to burn a body so big.

"Isn't this what you told me about, though? In the ancient rites, where witches dance naked in the grove about a holy fire?"

He'd remembered. "In the ancient rites, the priestesses drank a lot of mead before they danced naked. And at Midwinter, they didn't dance alone. They had partners…to…warm them…" Her face warmed with an unusually hot blush.

"While the fire burns, I will warm you," Chase said, reaching into the handcart. He pulled out a pair of blankets and a jug of mead. He handed her the jug, then spread the blankets on the ground. The flames reflected in his eyes made it seem almost as though the fire burned within him. He lay her down on the blankets, then knelt before her, lifting her legs up onto his shoulders so that her skirt fell back, baring her to him. She could feel the heat of him, ready to enter her, yet he did not. "But only if you want me. Do you?" he asked, his tone so gentle it could melt the iciest heart.

As she looked up into his eyes, she knew her heart had more than melted.

In the sacred grove, before the watching eyes of the forest gods, she could only speak the truth. Truth that had dawned on her tonight, as she lay naked in his arms. "Yes. More than any man I have ever known, I love you, and I will love you until I draw my last breath." Tears sprang to her eyes. "Even when spring comes and you run off to find your princess once more, I will love you still." Such was the life of a priestess. Always a lover, never a wife.

"You wish for me to stay here, with you?"

Rosa closed her eyes, wishing she could stop the tears from falling. "Yes. With all my heart."

"But your heart and soul belong here, to the forest."

She wept. "Yes. As priestess to the gods of the forest, my body and soul belong here, to them. I can never leave. But my heart belongs to you. Only you."

"Good. Because I think you stole my heart the moment you first looked at me, and I will never love any other woman the way I love you."

At his words, her eyes flew open, staring at him, but he thrust deep inside her, and she could do little more than moan at the pleasure of it. This was nothing like the first time, or the second. Every thrust was slow and deep, like the beat of a giant heart at the centre of her world. Somehow, he'd unlaced her dress, letting her breasts spill out, and his hands were warm as he caressed her, never once changing his pace.

The world spun and stood still, air freezing her flesh even as his skin heated it to burning, while the fire within her built and built, a blaze she could not contain.

And when she screamed out, "YES!" as the pleasure of their union overwhelmed her, it seemed the whole forest shouted with her.

# Forty-One

A thousand voices whispered, debating whether they should wake him up, remind him of his duties, or let him sleep a little longer.

Chase's heart sank. He'd fallen asleep in the Great Hall again, his head pillowed on something so soft it might be a maiden's breast. He didn't want to wake to find out what it really was, for he wanted to dream a little longer, about the magical maiden who summoned such a fire inside him, he could not resist her. Especially when her ice-blue eyes had glowed with some enchantment, enticing him to take what was so freely given…

He had to wake now, for his cock was far too alert for such a public place.

Chase dared to open his eyes. A pink nipple sat before him, like a berry atop sweet, creamy flesh, begging to be tasted.

"Serve your priestess, knight."

"Yesss, the High Priestess."

"You swore to serve."

Hissing whispers came from all around, but he saw no one. Trees stood sentinel on either side, their branches meeting above, like he lay in a massive cathedral.

With a lovely young woman. Rosa, the priestess of the forest.

He tried to lift his hand to stroke her hair off her face, but he could not. One arm was tucked beneath her, holding her tight to him, while his other hand was trapped between her thighs, with only his thumb free. He moved his thumb experimentally, eliciting a gasp from Rosa.

He pressed with the pad of his thumb, and it slipped inside her, her irresistible heat contracting around him just as she had last night.

His cock was now rock hard, as though he hadn't touched a woman in years, when he knew he'd made love to this one scant hours before.

"Yes," Rosa whispered, and a thousand voices agreed with her.

She shifted, rolling him onto his back so that she could sit astride him, her heat engulfing him completely. Her breasts, bouncing free of her unlaced bodice, taunted him.

He sat up, needing to kiss her, to taste those creamy breasts, to match the timing of her rocking hips with thrusts of his own.

"Yesss…"

"YES!"

"Yessss…"

"Oh, yes."

A thousand voices echoed his thoughts, until he and Rosa cried out in shared pleasure for a moment that seemed to last for ever…but not long enough.

When he could see clearly enough to look around, they were alone in the cathedral clearing, beside the ashes of last night's pyre, wrapped in her red cloak, on the forest floor.

"Hail the new High Priestess, for she has conquered the fire god himself in the sacred grove," a smug whisper hissed.

"Who said that?" Chase demanded, looking around.

Rosa blinked. "You heard that, too?"

"Of course. Now, show yourself!" Chase commanded.

"The knight cannot see."

"He sees only the High Priestess."

"So nubile is she."

Hissing laughter drowned out the rest of the words echoing around them.

Rosa ducked her head, no longer meeting his eyes as she laced up her bodice. "I should return to the house and wash." She levered herself up off Chase's lap, and cold air rushed to cool what ardour he had left. "You should…go to the Baron to collect your reward."

Chase cleaned up as best he could, and rose. "Not without you."

She shook her head. "I have no need of

coin, and I don't think Alard wants to see me. But you will surely need it, wherever you are going."

Chase folded his arms across his chest. "I'm going home, with my wife."

Rosa froze, her face losing all colour. "You never said...never mentioned...a wife." Tears filled her eyes.

No, she could not cry. Not now. Not after...

He rushed to take her in his arms. "My lady, please do not cry. If I've done things wrong, I must make amends. Tell me again how the ancient marriage rite goes. I will do it all over, until I have it right."

Her words were muffled in the folds of his shirt, but he could still make them out. "The couple would come to the altar, and pledge their love before witnesses. Then, they would spend the night in the sacred grove, to receive the gods' blessing on their union..."

"And the priestesses. How was it different for them?" Chase prompted.

"Only the High Priestess was permitted to marry, in a secret ceremony witnessed by the gods and those who served them, at Midwinter. The couple were allowed to drink nothing but Midwinter's Night mead, for they take the role of the winter goddess and the god of fire, uniting to drive away the cold and renew the land for another year. The couple were not truly married unless the gods found them worthy, by showing the couple a sign at dawn, which is why the priestess often married one of the fire god's priests..." Rosa stared at him. "But you can't have meant to marry me. You're leaving."

"I told you, I'm not going anywhere without you, and you wanted me to stay, Lady Rosa."

"I'm not a lady. Just a village witch, and maybe a priestess. Nothing more. Chase, you could have married some princess or fine lady. Why would you tie yourself to someone like me?"

"Because I love you, and I don't want some princess, or anyone else. I want you as my wife, Lady Rosa, which you are because you are a knight's lady. I pledged my life to you the first time you saved my life. And then you saved me again last night...so I am doubly indebted to you. A debt I will happily take a lifetime to repay." He took her hands in one of his, tilting her chin up with his other hand so that he might look into her eyes. "My lovely Lady Rosa, High Priestess to all the gods of the forest, will you accept a poor knight as your husband, to love and serve you until my last breath?"

Please say yes, he thought but did not say. Would it help if he dropped to his knees and begged?

"She already said yes."

"Several times."

"He was too busy between her thighs."

"Yes!"

More hissing laughter.

"Silence! I would hear her answer, not yours!" Chase snapped.

Silence fell.

A giggle escaped from Rosa. "I don't think anyone has ever told the gods of the forest to be quiet before. Only the High Priestess is meant to hear them, and even then, I thought it might be something my grandmother made up. How you can hear them, too...I do not know."

"Maybe it's the sign of the gods' favour, like you spoke of. Please, Rosa. An answer, I beg you."

The trees seemed to lean in, as though they wanted to hear, too.

She laughed. "Yes, yes, a thousand times yes! Especially if it means that last night won't be the only time we make love."

"I sure hope not!" Chase wadded up the blankets and tossed them into the hand cart, followed by the empty mead jug. "I plan on warming your bed for many nights to come, Lady Rosa, if you are willing."

Rosa tucked her arm under his. "I think I will grow accustomed to having you in my bed far faster than I will learn to like being Lady anything. But first, I'd like to cook my new husband a wedding breakfast. Something for stamina, and strength, washed down with something to sweeten his tongue…"

Laughing, they ambled through the forest for home.

# Forty-Two

"And...I think she's full," Rosa said as her nipple popped out of baby Maja's mouth.

While she retied the laces of her gown, Chase carried the sleeping baby over to the cradle she shared with her twin sister, Saskia, for the girls screamed fit to wake the dead if they were parted for long.

"Do you think they'll sleep through the night?" Chase asked doubtfully, smoothing a blanket over the girls.

"My sleeping spells have worked fine so far. They will not wake until sunrise, even if they weren't full to bursting with milk." She lifted her lips for a kiss. "We have all night, the longest night of the year."

"We'll need it. We've scarcely shared a bed, even to sleep, since the girls were born," Chase grumbled as he threw a couple of blankets over his shoulder. He fastened his cloak, then picked up the two jugs of mead from the table. "Which barrel is this?"

"The Midwinter's Night mead, strong and sweet, like you, made the night you first touched my heart," Rosa said, settling her red cloak across her shoulders.

"The night I touched your breast in my sleep, you mean."

"I'd like to think the gods guided your hand," she said lightly, slipping her arm through the handle of a basket of food she'd packed to sustain them through the night. Outside, the trees whispered, as if a high wind whipped through their branches, but the night was still. "Can you still hear them?"

Chase closed the door behind him and squinted up at the trees. "Unfortunately, yes. They've been whispering all day. Your gods of the forest are randier than I am, and that's saying something."

Rosa set off with a skip in her step. "Then perhaps we should hurry to the grove, so I can help you with that."

Chase followed, but Rosa was faster, reaching the unlit bonfire first.

"Oh, it's beautiful," she whispered. Chase had edged the altar in holly and mistletoe, with a row of lit candles on both ends. "I should have thought to bring an offering, too."

Chase touched his torch to the bonfire. "Your gods of the forest were very clear about what they desire from their High Priestess."

"They told you, but not me?"

"You were busy inside with the girls. Too busy to listen to a bunch of randy trees who have taken a distinctly unholy shine to their High Priestess."

A shiver of alarm touched her. "Chase, you should not mock the gods of the forest so. If they struck you down for your insolence, I would be inconsolable. And the girls…"

"Do not fear. I may not worship your gods as devoutly as you do, but we have an understanding. As long as I keep you happy." Chase untied the laces of her gown, then pushed it down, until it puddled on the ground. The two woollen shifts she wore beneath soon followed it. Then he lifted her so she perched on the edge of the altar, well away from the holly and candles, and peeled her hose and boots off her dangling legs.

Rosa pulled the edges of her cloak closed over her nakedness. "What are you doing? We can't do this on the altar!"

"That's not what they say!" Chase raised his arms, waving at the treetops.

Now Rosa could hear their hissed words, and what she did hear made her blush.

Surely the god of fire hadn't dared bend a goddess over her own altar to take her from behind…

"Yes!"

"Please!"

"Drink the nectar of the gods, High Priestess!"

Behind Rosa, the bonfire finally caught, roaring up with a wave of heat that enticed her to loosen her hold on her cloak. She reached for Chase's golden cup, brimful of mead, and drank half of it in one draught, before handing it to Chase to finish.

Then Chase stripped off, until he stood before her in nothing but his white wolf-fur cloak. Only then did he position himself between her thighs, ready.

She lifted her glowing ice-blue eyes to meet his fiery gaze. "Oh, Sir Knight, what a big sword you have."

"All the better to...gods, it feels so good to be inside you again, my lady!"

# About the Author

Demelza Carlton has always loved the ocean, but on her first snorkelling trip she found she was afraid of fish.

She has since swum with sea lions, sharks and sea cucumbers and stood on spray drenched cliffs over a seething sea as a seven-metre cyclonic swell surged in, shattering a shipwreck below.

Demelza now lives in Perth, Western Australia, the shark attack capital of the world.

The *Ocean's Gift* series was her first foray into fiction, followed by her suspense thriller *Nightmares* trilogy. She swears the *Mel Goes to Hell* series ambushed her on a crowded train and wouldn't leave her alone.

Want to know more? You can follow Demelza on Facebook, Twitter, YouTube or her website, Demelza Carlton's Place at:

www.demelzacarlton.com

# Books by Demelza Carlton

## Siren of Secrets series

Ocean's Secret (#1)

Ocean's Gift (#2)

Ocean's Infiltrator (#3)

## Siren of War series

Ocean's Justice (#1)

Ocean's Widow (#2)

Ocean's Bride (#3)

Ocean's Rise (#4)

Ocean's War (#5)

How To Catch Crabs

## Nightmares Trilogy

Nightmares of Caitlin Lockyer (#1)

Necessary Evil of Nathan Miller (#2)

Afterlife of Alana Miller (#3)

## Mel Goes to Hell series

Welcome to Hell (#1)

See You in Hell (#2)

Mel Goes to Hell (#3)

To Hell and Back (#4)

The Holiday From Hell (#5)

All Hell Breaks Loose (#6)

## Romance Island Resort series

Maid for the Rock Star (#1)
The Rock Star's Email Order Bride (#2)
The Rock Star's Virginity (#3)
The Rock Star and the Billionaire (#4)
The Rock Star Wants A Wife (#5)
The Rock Star's Wedding (#6)
Maid for the South Pole (#7)
Jailbird Bride (#8)

## Romance a Medieval Fairytale series

Enchant: Beauty and the Beast Retold
Dance: Cinderella Retold
Fly: Goose Girl Retold
Revel: Twelve Dancing Princesses Retold
Silence: Little Mermaid Retold
Awaken: Sleeping Beauty Retold
Embellish: Brave Little Tailor Retold
Appease: Princess and the Pea Retold
Blow: Three Little Pigs Retold
Return: Hansel and Gretel Retold
Wish: Aladdin Retold
Melt: Snow Queen Retold
Spin: Rumpelstiltskin Retold
Kiss: Frog Prince Retold
Hunt: Red Riding Hood Retold
Reflect: Snow White Retold
Roar: Goldilocks Retold
Cobble: Elves and the Shoemaker Retold

Made in the USA
Coppell, TX
27 January 2021

48857734R00154